D0442913

REVENGE OF
SUPERSTITION
MOUNTAIN

BOOK THREE

REVENGE OF SUPERSTITION MOUNTAIN

BOOK THREE

ELISE BROACH

ILLUSTRATED BY
OLGA AND ALEKSEY IVANOV

Christy Ottaviano Books
Henry Holt and Company
New York

Henry Holt and Company, LLC
Publishers since 1866
175 Fifth Avenue
New York, New York 10010
mackids.com

Henry Holt books may be purchased for business or promotional use. For information
on bulk purchases, please contact Macmillan Corporate and Premium Sales Department
at (800) 221-7945 x5442 or by e-mail at specialmarkets@macmillan.com.

Library of Congress Cataloging-in-Publication Data
Broach, Elise.
Revenge of Superstition Mountain / Elise Broach ; illustrated by
Aleksey and Olga Ivanov.
pages cm
Sequel to: Missing on Superstition Mountain.
Summary: The Barker brothers and their friend Delilah secretly climb up to
Superstition Mountain one last time, hoping to solve the remaining mysteries,
including whether the librarian is really the ghost of Julia Thomas,
what was their uncle Hank's role in discovering the gold mine,
and especially, who is trying to kill them.
ISBN 978-0-8050-8909-7 (hardback)
ISBN 978-1-250-05686-3 (paperback)
ISBN 978-1-62779-238-7 (e-book)
[1. Mountains—Fiction. 2. Brothers—Fiction. 3. Superstition
Mountains (Ariz.)—Fiction. 4. Arizona—Fiction. 5. Mystery and
detective stories.] I. Ivanov, O. (Olga), illustrator. II. Ivanov, A. (Aleksey),
illustrator. III. Title.
PZ7.B78083Rev 2014 [Fic]—dc23   2014005283

First Edition—2014

Printed in the United States of America
by R. R. Donnelley & Sons Company, Harrisonburg, Virginia

1 3 5 7 9 10 8 6 4 2

For my friend Carol Sheriff and her children,
Anna Daileader Sheriff and Benjamin Daileader
Sheriff—excellent readers, all
—E. B.

REVENGE OF SUPERSTITION MOUNTAIN

BOOK THREE

CHAPTER 1
A SECRET MEETING

"WHAT WAS THAT?"

The librarian's voice cut through the cool night air, and Simon shot Henry a quick, silencing glance.

They were huddled against the rough concrete wall of the library building, in the shrubbery below the open window, with Delilah and Jack wedged up against them in a tangle of elbows and knees. Twigs and leaves scratched their faces. As usual when Henry was desperate to keep perfectly still and quiet, he was beset with discomforts. He suddenly had to go to the bathroom; his legs itched; he felt sure he was about to sneeze. The more he considered how terrible it would be if he did sneeze, the more he felt a sneeze welling up inside him.

It had been Simon's idea to eavesdrop on the August meeting of the Superstition Historical Society, to hear

firsthand what the treasure hunters were up to. On the other side of the window, the meeting had just ended, and the librarian Julia Thomas, president of the historical society, had asked the members of the executive committee to remain behind. From what Henry could tell, after the scrape of chairs and murmur of departing voices, there were only three people left in the room: the creepy librarian, Officer Myers—the big, stern policeman who had first warned the boys to stay away from Superstition Mountain—and a man they figured had to be Richard Delgado, the caretaker at the cemetery, who was the historical society's secretary and whose addled daughter Sara was living proof of the mountain's eerie grip. A year ago, she had returned from its wilds in a fugue state, frightened and talking nonsensically. To Henry, it seemed like she had left the saner part of herself somewhere in the mountain's caves and canyons . . . with the bones of the people who'd died or disappeared there while searching for the Lost Dutchman's gold mine.

The gold mine! Even now, crouched in a sweaty human tangle under the screen of branches, Henry could picture the gold. He remembered its breathtaking luster in the dark mine, sparkling in the beam of the flashlight. It was the secret that he, Simon, Jack, and Delilah had kept all summer long: they had found the Lost Dutchman's Mine! The treasure that person after person had climbed Superstition Mountain in the hopes of finding, for over a century.

Of course, once the avalanche buried the mine's entrance, it was impossible to know if anyone would ever see the gold again. Simon, Henry, and Jack had barely managed to escape, and only because of Delilah's warning. But in the moments before the cascade of boulders thundered down the canyon wall, Jack had grabbed a fistful of sparkly golden flakes . . . and this was the sole remnant of their discovery. For the past month, he had kept them safe in an Altoids tin under his dresser, and sometimes, when the boys were playing a game in his room, he would take out the tin and wave it imperiously under the noses of his brothers, reminding them that he was the only one with real, actual gold from the Lost Dutchman's Mine. Then Simon would produce the gold nugget from the old Spanish saddlebag that Henry and Delilah had found in the canyon, and a heated argument would ensue about which was more valuable, the single nugget or the collection of golden flakes.

It was good they had those bits of gold, Henry thought. Sometimes during the long, hot sweep of the

summer—while Delilah's broken leg healed and the boys spent their days playing games with her or riding their bikes or keeping track of Josie, who was determinedly independent even for a cat—it had been hard to believe the gold was real. The gold mine was a secret; they could tell no one. It seemed not just separate from but at odds with the rest of their daily lives in the tiny town of Superstition, in the home the Barker family had inherited a few months ago from Mr. Barker's cattle-wrangling, poker-playing, adventure-loving uncle, Hank Cormody, who had died in his eighties after a long, eventful life. Uncle Hank was a former U.S. Cavalry scout and the relative for whom Henry had been named—in what he sometimes felt was a cruel joke designed to make him painfully aware of all the ways in which he was not brave, exciting, and adventurous.

But Mr. Barker had idolized his uncle and loved telling stories about him, and throughout their childhoods the boys had a special place in their hearts for their great-uncle Hank, even though they had met him only a handful of times and barely knew him. He sent them funny birthday cards and inappropriate presents (like a shiny silver cap gun for Henry's birthday, which Mrs. Barker had promptly confiscated), and every once in a long while he burst into their lives for Thanksgiving or a holiday weekend, brimming with jokes and tales about his life in the West. Sometimes Henry felt he didn't so much know Uncle Hank as know *of* Uncle Hank. But nonetheless, the impression was a vivid one, of flowing white hair, a booming voice, and hands patterned with interesting calluses and scars.

The Barkers had moved to Uncle Hank's brown, shingled house in Superstition in June, at the end of kindergarten for Jack, and fourth grade for Henry, and fifth grade for Simon. They had met Delilah, who was Henry's age, shortly afterward. Henry could scarcely believe all that had happened to them since then, over the course of the long summer, in the shadow of the great, spooky mountain whose essential mystery they had yet to solve.

So here they all were, frozen beneath the screen of leaves and branches outside the library window, listening and trying not to be heard. Henry felt like Harriet the Spy, the main character from one of the books he loved. He wished he had a notebook to transcribe the conversation flowing through the window.

"What do you mean? I didn't hear anything," a man's voice said, and Henry recognized it as belonging to Officer Myers.

"Something outside," Julia Thomas replied. Heels clicked against the floor, approaching the window, and a man's heavier footsteps followed. Beneath the twiggy canopy, Henry held his breath, and he saw Jack's eyes grow wide.

"Do you see anything out there?" the librarian asked.

"No. You're getting paranoid, Julia." The voices were now above their heads, floating through the thin night air. After a minute, the footsteps left the window.

"I'm not paranoid, I'm careful. Which is more than I can say for you and Richard. That rock slide was your fault! We may have lost our only chance of getting to the gold."

Henry gasped. "They started the avalanche," he whispered.

"I thought so," Simon answered softly. "They were watching us the whole time. That means they know where the gold mine is."

Delilah tensed. "They could have gotten us killed."

"Yeah," Jack repeated, "KILLED." In the dark beneath the bushes, Henry could see him clench his fists.

Beyond the windowsill, the three adults were now arguing.

"I told you, my foot slipped," Henry heard Richard Delgado say testily. "I had no way of knowing that would bring down half the mountain!"

"You should have watched where you were stepping," Mrs. Thomas snapped. "The gold mine is buried behind a wall of rock now."

"Hang on," Officer Myers interrupted. "Who says that was the gold mine? We have no idea what the kids found in there. For all we know, it was just a cave."

Mrs. Thomas answered curtly, "No. It's the Lost Dutchman's Mine. I'm certain of it. And now that we know those children are after the gold, we have to move quickly."

Beneath the bushes, Henry squirmed, rubbing the back of his hand against his nose.

"What's the matter?" Delilah whispered, watching him.

"I think I might sneeze," Henry whispered back.

Simon shook his head. "Well, don't. Shhhhh, this is important."

Through the window, the debate continued. "Then what do you want to do?" Mr. Delgado asked. "As you said, if it is the gold mine, it's buried under a mound of boulders."

"We can either try to break through the boulders or find another way in," the librarian answered.

"You'd need dynamite to break up those rocks," Officer Myers said. "And it would be pretty hard to have an explosion up there in the canyon and keep it a secret."

Mr. Delgado mumbled his agreement. "What about your other idea? The gold from the mine that might still be somewhere near town—the nuggets that Jacob Waltz took and kept in a candle box under his bed. You said he might have left the candle box with the neighbor lady when he died—why don't we work on finding that?" He paused. "It's a lot easier than going up the mountain again. And safer. That place is . . ." His voice trailed off.

Henry turned to Delilah. Box of gold? They had heard the story of Jacob Waltz and the gold mine from their geologist friend Emmett Trask. Back in the late 1880s, when the old miner was being cared for on his deathbed by his neighbor, the original Julia Thomas, he supposedly gave her directions to the mine, and maybe even a map . . . but this was the first Henry had heard about a box of gold under the bed. The directions to the mine had survived on a scrap of paper the children had found in Uncle Hank's desk, in the hidden compartment of his orange metal coin box . . . written by someone other than Uncle Hank.

Mrs. Thomas sounded impatient. "The deathbed ore? Because as I told you, we have no idea where to begin to look for that. Some believe that he didn't give it to Julia at all. That it was stolen by someone when she left Waltz's deathbed to get a doctor, and he died while she was gone."

"People have been looking for that deathbed ore forever," Officer Myers interjected. "But what about the ghost town? We know she stayed there before and after her trip up the mountain to look for the gold."

The ghost town! Henry remembered the desolate silence of Gold Creek, with its row of ramshackle buildings . . . and the shattered floorboards of the Black Cat Saloon, where Simon had fallen, disappearing into a cellar where something or someone had lain in wait for him.

"Yes, the ghost town," Mr. Delgado echoed. "That's exactly where we should be looking. At the old hotel, where she stayed with those German brothers. What if they left something behind?"

Simon nudged Henry. "See? We have to go back," he whispered. "Before they do."

Henry opened his mouth to agree, but suddenly the sneeze he'd been suppressing burbled up into his throat and his nose. He sucked in his breath, trying to swallow it, but something—part sneeze, part breath, part sputter—escaped.

Ahhhhh-phhhht!

Simon, Jack, and Delilah stared at him in horror.

Inside the room, a chair scraped the floor, and heels came clicking furiously toward the window.

"That!" Julia Thomas exclaimed. "Do you hear it now? There's someone outside the window."

CHAPTER 2
COMMOTION

A RIPPLE OF PANIC SHOOK the bushes. Henry didn't know what to do. If Mrs. Thomas looked closely enough through the leaves, she would see them. There wasn't time to get away. He could tell from the stricken expressions on the others' faces that they were making the same desperate calculation. The librarian's fast-clicking heels had almost reached the window above them. Henry crouched as low to the ground as he could, waiting in horror for the moment he knew was coming.

Then, just as Mrs. Thomas's bright polished nails curled over the windowsill, there was a rustle of branches. Henry saw a dark shape sail over the bushes. It landed with a feather-soft thud on the sill.

Josie!

How did *she* get there? Through the thatch of twigs and leaves, Henry could see her balancing, all four paws on the sill, as the librarian's hands jerked back in surprise. Josie's back arched, and her fur rose in a spiky shroud. Her ears flattened against her head. Face-to-face with Julia Thomas, she yowled her displeasure.

"What in the world!" The librarian recoiled, backing away from the window.

"It's just a cat," Officer Myers said. "Calm down." He crossed the room and slammed the window shut, as Josie leapt to the ground, streaking off into the night.

Henry's rigid shoulders collapsed in relief.

"Sheesh!" Simon hissed at him. "That could have been a disaster."

"Well, he did say he was going to sneeze," Delilah whispered.

"That creepy librarian almost saw us!" Jack chimed in disapprovingly.

Henry cringed. "Sorry," he mumbled. "I tried to stop it."

With a glance at him, Delilah changed the subject. "What was going on with Josie?"

"She must have followed us," Simon said.

"I know, but I mean the way she freaked out. I've never seen her do that."

Jack nodded. "She hates that creepy librarian as much as we do!"

"But she's never even seen her before," Henry said thoughtfully. It would be nice to believe that Josie was an excellent judge of character, but through long years of experience, the Barkers knew this was not the case. Josie tended to like people who were quiet, slow, and neat and, most important, who didn't pay any attention to her. She was particularly drawn to people who didn't like animals at all. Back when they lived in Chicago, Henry remembered how Josie would settle herself in the lap of their neighbor Mrs. Crichter, an easily irritated woman who often knocked on the door to complain about how loud the boys were in the backyard or how inconvenient it was when one of their balls flew over her fence. When Josie leapt onto her lap, Mrs. Crichter would flinch in disgust, complain about shedding, and demand that someone take her away. Josie, meanwhile, adored her. Henry thought that it would be very hard to like someone who didn't like you back. It reminded him of one time last year when he had tried to be friends with a boy who was much cooler and more popular than Henry at school, and how it had only made him feel bad about himself. But clearly, it didn't bother Josie at all.

"She looked the way she does when there's a dog coming at her," Simon said. That was right, Henry thought. There was a goofy boxer down the street in Chicago who had sometimes bothered Josie, and she would react with that same dramatic posture, a mixture of fright and fury.

Simon cocked his head and turned toward the square of white light shining through the window. The voices behind the glass had faded to a muted murmur.

"We might as well go home," he said. "We told Mom and Dad we'd be back by nine, and we can't hear anything now anyway."

"What were they saying about the ghost town?" Delilah asked.

"They're going there to look for the gold that Jacob Waltz gave to Julia Thomas when he died. Or for something that will lead them to it," Simon explained. "Which means we have to get there first."

"But what about—" Henry shivered, thinking of the broken floorboards in the Black Cat Saloon, where Simon had tumbled into the dark cellar.

"We'll be careful, Hen," Simon told him. "We know what to watch out for this time."

Privately, Henry thought that they never seemed to know what to watch out for; in fact, wasn't that the whole problem? Librarians who looked like people who'd lived a century ago; gunshots in a hidden canyon; a tombstone with their own name written across it; rattlesnakes and rock slides; a ghost-town cellar where something or someone had been waiting, and had rustled slowly through the blackness toward Simon.

"Let's go," Simon ordered, "and be QUIET! We don't want them nosing around again."

Carefully, he pulled aside a web of branches and extricated himself from the shrubbery, brushing bits of leaves and dirt from his legs. Jack tumbled after him, not nearly so quietly, and then Henry and Delilah followed.

They ran around the corner to the shadowy back of the library building, where they had stashed their bikes in a landscape bed. As Delilah raced ahead, Henry thought what a relief it was to have her out of her cast. She could keep up with them again.

Delilah seemed to be thinking the same thing. "I can go to the ghost town with you this time," Delilah said to

Henry, smiling as she threw her leg over the pink chrome bar of her bicycle. "I can't wait, after all you told me."

Henry was thinking that he himself could wait, especially after Simon's encounter with that thing in the cellar.

CHAPTER 3

PLOTS AND PLOTTING

THEY SAID GOOD-BYE to Delilah at the corner of her block, then pedaled hard toward home. Their house—Uncle Hank's house—waited at the end of the street, the porch light casting a pale, reassuring circle of light across the scrubby yard. The dry landscape still took Henry by surprise at times—the hardness of it, the tall fingers of saguaro cactuses, the bright bursts of desert flowers in a place that seemed so bare and harsh. Sometimes, the boys played moon landing in their backyard, behind the thin border of trees that separated their house from the rolling foothills of Superstition Mountain. They would disembark from their wagon spacecraft to the rocky lunar surface with a bunch of old jars, to explore and collect samples (which usually involved Jack trapping lizards and pretending they were aliens bent on destruction). Henry had to admit, unlike when they had played the game in the verdant lawns of their Chicago neighborhood, here in Arizona it really did feel like they had landed on the moon. But as strange a place as Superstition was, during the hot stretch of summer, it had started to feel more and more familiar. Henry thought about Illinois only rarely now, and when he did, it was almost never with a sense of wistfulness or longing. He realized to his surprise that Uncle Hank's house had become home.

As they rode up to the open garage, Josie darted past them into the dark backyard, amber eyes glowing.

"There's Josie," Jack yelled.

"She looks back to normal," Simon observed.

"Josie," Henry called to her, stopping his bike. He reached out his hand, snapping his fingers. Josie hesitated on the lip of the yard. But she only studied him impassively for a moment before slipping into the night.

Mr. Barker was in the kitchen, finishing the dishes, when they bounded through the door from the garage.

"Hey, guys," he said cheerily. "How's the night air?"

The boys looked at each other. Mr. Barker often asked goofy questions like this, for which there was no real answer. Simon shrugged. "It's nice out."

"Not nearly as hot as it is during the day, right?" Mr. Barker said. "It's a better time for you to be outside."

That was certainly true, Henry thought. The baking heat of summer in Arizona meant you couldn't ever go barefoot outside; the pavement fried your feet. During the day, the boys were thirsty all the time, and because Mrs. Barker was annoyingly insistent about sun lotion, their skin smelled constantly of tropical fruits. Riding their bikes or playing in the yard at night was pure relief by comparison. The temperature dropped twenty degrees or more. When the cool night air beckoned, anything seemed possible.

Henry heard voices on the deck, and Aunt Kathy's telltale rolling laugh. "Aunt Kathy's here?"

"Yes, she came to see Emmett for the weekend, and they stopped by on their way back from the airport." Mr. Barker finished rinsing a saucepan and balanced it in the dish rack, then wiped his hands on his shorts. "It's almost time for bed, but you guys can go out and say a quick hello."

"She's ALWAYS here now," Jack declared, already thundering to the sliding door and yanking it open.

Aunt Kathy had been visiting Arizona almost weekly since she met Emmett Trask. He was her new boyfriend, she proudly told the boys, and such a sweetie. Very responsible and thoughtful, but interestingly independent, which she liked . . . and her worries that his work as a geologist had turned him into a nerdy loner had happily proven to be unfounded. Her frequent visits were a nice bonus for the Barker boys, because (1) Aunt Kathy was a lot of fun, (2) Emmett knew a lot about Superstition Mountain, and since he was often at their house now, that made him conveniently available to answer their questions, and (3) their parents were distracted by adult conversations and the tasks of entertaining, which meant the boys had more freedom than usual, especially in the evenings.

Henry and Simon followed Jack onto the deck, where their mother was sitting at the patio table with Emmett and Aunt Kathy.

"Boys!" Aunt Kathy cried. "I was hoping you'd come home before we had to leave." She hugged Jack against her side, ruffled Henry's curls, and then reached over to squeeze Simon's arm.

Emmett stood up and grinned at them. "I was hoping I'd see you too. I had a meeting in Phoenix last week, and I had a chance to go to that cemetery where Jacob Waltz's neighbor, Julia Thomas, is buried."

"You DID?" Jack yelled.

"Jack, shhhh," Mrs. Barker hushed. "The whole neighborhood will hear you."

"Is she really buried there?" Henry asked, while Simon blurted, "Did you find her grave?"

"Yes, yes, and yes," Emmett answered, holding up his hands against their barrage of questions. "I talked to the groundskeeper, and he showed me the map of grave plots. Then I walked out to the actual grave. It's there, with a marker. The dates are correct . . . and as I told you, Phoenix was where she lived until the end of her life, and where she died. Do you remember me telling you about the weird cult she was involved in? Burning fire pits in the yard, and other strange rituals?"

Henry did vaguely remember this. It had seemed spooky when Emmett described it before, almost like witchcraft, and it made the original Julia Thomas seem even more unknowable.

"Well, her house is no longer standing," Emmett continued, "but I drove through that part of town on my way back to the freeway. It's not far from where she's buried."

"What did it say on her tombstone?" Henry asked. In his mind's eye, he could see the tilted stone markers in the neglected, older section of the Superstition cemetery, and the one with Julia Elena Thomas's name carved in faded letters across the rough face. With a shudder, he recalled the tombstone that bore their own last name: BARKER. He knew that Delilah must have seen her own name on a tombstone too, when her father was buried, and the thought made him feel hollow inside. Seeing BARKER on a tombstone had been awful because there was no explanation for it; but for Delilah, seeing DUNWORTHY on a tombstone must have been awful because there *was* an explanation.

"Just her name, Julia Thomas Schaffer," Emmett answered, and at Henry's puzzled expression, he added, "Remember how she married Albert Schaffer later on? After she divorced her first husband, Emil Thomas. And the tombstone also had the dates of her birth and death. She died in 1917, on her birthday, actually."

Henry flinched. It seemed terrible to die on your own birthday. But then he wondered if maybe it felt like an accomplishment, because you'd made it to a whole year older.

"So, I don't know what you guys saw at the cemetery," Emmett was saying, "but it couldn't have been her grave."

"The cemetery?" Mrs. Barker looked at Henry sharply. "Were you boys at the cemetery?"

Henry bit his lip and turned to Simon. It was sometimes hard to keep track of what their parents did and didn't know about their adventures over the summer. It was exhausting to keep secrets from them, and it plagued him with guilt. But the events of the summer were like a row of dominoes; the boys couldn't reveal one without a chain reaction of other revelations, and there was still so much about the mountain and Uncle Hank's search for the gold that they didn't understand.

Simon answered her smoothly. "Yeah, sometimes we ride our bikes over there 'cuz it's away from the busy roads. It has this really cool historic part, with graves from the 1800s."

"Isn't that interesting!" Aunt Kathy exclaimed. "So you can find out who lived around here all those years ago . . . the pioneers and settlers. Is your Uncle Hank buried there?"

"Nope," Mr. Barker said. "He was cremated. We have his ashes—"

"Jim," Mrs. Barker cautioned. Henry thought, not for the first time, that his parents were an odd combination.

As a medical illustrator, Mrs. Barker spent her days studying and then rendering in pencil sketch or water-color the most visceral images of human body parts, often riddled with disease or maimed by injury. The boys could ask her about anything, the more graphic and disgusting the better. But she had a clear sense of what was appropriate, by age, by timing, and for certain company. Their father, on the other hand, was squeamish to the point of nausea about even mundane things like splinters, yet he was outrageously blunt about what their mother called inappropriate personal details that she herself would never share in polite company. Henry supposed that they balanced each other out, and that maybe this was what you did when you chose somebody to marry—tried to find someone who could fill in your gaps.

Mrs. Barker regarded them skeptically. "Is it okay for you boys to wander around a place like that? It's not private property?"

Simon shrugged. "We didn't stay there for long. And nobody said anything to us."

"We talked to the daughter of the guy who's in charge of the cemetery," Henry added. "And she didn't tell us to leave or anything." Of course, Sara Delgado wasn't actually in a state to communicate any coherent messages, Henry thought.

"I think it's fine as long as they don't disturb the graves," Emmett said. "But at any rate, whatever marker you saw in the cemetery, it couldn't have been for this Julia Thomas. She's buried in Phoenix."

"Thanks for checking on that for us," Henry said.

"Yeah," Simon added, his brow furrowing. "That saves us some time."

"What do you mean?" Mrs. Barker looked from Simon to Henry and back again. "Time for what?"

But Aunt Kathy was finished with the cemetery discussion. "You boys are very polite, do you know that?" She turned to Emmett. "Did you hear how they said thank you? Without even being prompted! My sister has done such a good job of raising them."

Emmett's cheeks reddened, though Henry couldn't tell whether he was embarrassed for the boys or for himself. "Yes, she has."

Mrs. Barker smiled, while Mr. Barker did a mock double take. "Hey! What am I? Chopped liver?"

Aunt Kathy laughed. "Of course not! I mean BOTH of

you. You're both such good parents. I want to be just like you when I grow up." She winked at Henry.

Mrs. Barker stood up and slipped an arm around Jack's shoulders. "All right, boys," she said. "Time for bed. Go brush your teeth and I'll come tuck you in."

The boys fled the deck in relief.

In the bathroom, crowded around the sink, they discussed the trip to the ghost town.

"But what are we looking for?" Henry asked. "The stairs in the hotel were all rotted out. We can't get to the second floor where Julia Thomas stayed. And even if we could, you saw what those other buildings were like in the ghost town—hardly anything was left behind."

Simon looked exasperated. "Okay, number one, we don't have to know what we're looking for to find something interesting. Think about the saddlebag and the Spanish coins and the directions to the gold mine! Number two, we didn't really have a chance to poke around the hotel, 'cuz I fell through the floor right after we got there. Number three, you heard what Emmett told us about those people in the historical society: they're TREASURE hunters. They're looking for the gold. So if they think the ghost town is a good place to find it, that's where we need to go." He paused. "Before they do."

"Yeah!" Jack echoed, spitting a mouthful of toothpaste into the sink.

Henry sighed. Simon was so annoyingly logical. He had an answer for everything.

"Besides, Delilah is dying to go, and it wouldn't be fair to her not to," Simon added. "She missed it last time."

Missed what? Henry grumbled to himself. The terror of not knowing what was down in the dark cellar with Simon? The ordeal of trying to haul him up before it got him?

"When do you want to go?" Henry asked resignedly.

"Tomorrow!" Simon said. "The sooner the better." And then, seeing Henry's face, he added, "Don't worry, Hen. We'll be careful. This time we'll bring a rope and a flashlight."

And hope we don't need them, Henry thought grimly.

CHAPTER 4
RETURN TO GOLD CREEK

THE NEXT MORNING, the boys met Delilah at the corner of Waltz Street to ride out to the ghost town. It had been Delilah's job to check on the room numbers for Julia Thomas and the Petrasch brothers in the old hotel ledger that they had brought back from their first trip to the ghost town, so that they would know where to begin their search. As promised, Simon had gathered a rope, a flashlight, some granola bars, and several water bottles and stuffed them into his school backpack. He rode ahead with the straps looped over both shoulders, the pack bulging.

Henry realized that in a few weeks, with school starting, that same backpack would be filled with textbooks and papers. And they would all be at a new school, with an unfamiliar lunchroom and playground and hallways crowded with strangers. He decided he liked the backpack better the way it was now, fat and heavy with supplies for exploring.

Soon they had passed the streets of low bungalows and stucco ranch houses and were riding through the outskirts of town.

"Are you worried?" Delilah asked Henry, slowing down to pedal beside him. "Because of that thing in the cellar?"

Henry squinted over at her, hoping his brothers were out of earshot. "A little, I guess."

"Maybe it was nothing. Maybe something just fell over in the dark down there, and Simon couldn't see."

Henry shook his head. "No, it was moving. We heard it. It kept rustling."

"Do you think it was a snake?"

"I don't know. Whatever it was, if it lives down there, it must be getting food somehow."

"Well, we'll just have to be extra careful in that old hotel," Delilah said.

"Yeah," Henry said doubtfully. He felt glum. All this time, he had thought he was getting braver, more like Uncle Hank—on the mountain, in the gold mine—and now he felt just like his old anxious, fearful self. Maybe change was like that—not steady and reliable, but gradual, unpredictable, and full of setbacks . . . one step forward, two steps backward. Or maybe he hadn't really changed at all. Maybe you could never change your essential nature.

"Look! There's the cemetery!" Jack yelled, barreling past Simon into the lead.

Henry glanced through the wrought-iron gates at the rows of tombstones gleaming in the sun. It was strange to think of so many dead people gathered in one place, a crowd of skeletons in boxes underground. He thought of all these people as they must have been when they were alive, with their separate, busy lives; their families and jobs and houses; the books they must have read. It was impossible to imagine that the endpoint of all that *life* was this quiet, orderly place full of tombstones. From the road, he couldn't see the far corner where the older graves were, the markers that read JULIA ELENA THOMAS and BARKER. But even in the bright, ordinary sunshine, just knowing they were out there sent a chill through him.

They rode past Black Top Mesa, where Emmett lived, and along Peralta Way into the desert, with the shadowy cliffs of Superstition Mountain rising in the distance. There were no houses on the sides of the road now, only the endless stretches of dry, pebbly ground, speckled with low shrubs and cactuses—the paddle-shaped arms of prickly pear and the tall, straight fingers of the saguaro. Jack raced ahead, calling, "I see it! I see the ghost town!"

There, far across the rough fields, rose the dark huddle of buildings, like an animal crouched in the brush, waiting for them. Henry could see their sagging roofs, and the stark shape of the old wooden water tower rising above them.

"Wow," Delilah exclaimed. "How do we get to it?"

"There's a path on the side of the road," Simon told her.

"Is there anything left in the buildings?" Delilah asked Henry. "Furniture and stuff?"

Henry tried to remember what they'd seen in the dark, dilapidated wooden buildings. "Not much. There was some junk outside, and the hotel had that ledger and the room keys, so maybe it wasn't cleaned out like some of the other places."

"I hope not," Delilah said. "It would be cool to find something."

"Here's the path!" Jack bellowed, turning off the road and onto the rutted wagon trail that led to Gold Creek.

"Wait for us, Jack," Simon ordered. "Don't go into the hotel till we get there."

They rode toward the cluster of buildings, bumping over the uneven path, as dust clouded the air.

When he reached the side of the hotel, Jack skidded to a halt and leapt off his bike, dropping it against the splintered porch. Henry pedaled through the dry clumps of grass to join him, looking with trepidation at the faded sign hanging above the doorway, with its faint image of a cat.

"Is this it?" Delilah asked excitedly, leaning her bike next to Jack's and Simon's. "The Black Cat Hotel and Saloon?"

Henry nodded. Together, they followed Simon and Jack across the porch of the hotel. At the doorway, Simon grabbed Jack's shoulder. "Let me go first. And walk exactly where I do, okay?'

"Okay, okay," Jack said impatiently. "But you're the one who fell through the floor, not me."

Simon glowered at him and led the way into the hotel, stepping carefully along the wall, where the floor was solid.

Henry could see the rough edges of the hole in the floor where Simon had fallen. Below the broken wood was pure darkness.

"Let's have a look," Simon said. He slid his arms out of the backpack and set it gently against the wall, digging around for the flashlight.

CHAPTER 5

"WHAT KIND OF PLACE IS THIS?"

HENRY COULD FEEL HIS HEART quicken. "Simon . . . ," he began, but Simon was already crawling carefully across the wooden planks to the edge of the hole, shining his flashlight into the cellar.

Henry and Delilah stepped gingerly on the solid boards a few feet from the gash in the floor, and Jack scrambled next to Simon. "What do you see? Is there a SNAKE down there?"

"No . . ." Simon swung the flashlight back and forth, and the beam showed a dirt floor and a dark pile of burlap sacks. "Those are the sacks I was standing on, but I don't see anything else. I have an idea. Let's throw a granola bar down there. Maybe whatever it is will come out to eat it."

"That's a great idea," Jack cried. He scooted over to the backpack and grabbed a granola bar, ripping open the foil wrapper.

"Drop it on the sacks where we can see it," Simon told him.

"Wait," Delilah said. "We should crumble it up." She took the bar from Jack and crunched it in her hands, scattering the crumbs where Simon shone the flashlight, over the dark pile of sacks.

Henry hung back from the edge of the hole, watching with a mounting sense of dread.

Simon continued to swing the flashlight beam across the sacks. "Do you see anything?" he asked Henry.

Henry squinted into the darkness. "No," he said finally, relieved. It was quiet in the cellar. The granola crumbs were untouched. "Maybe whatever it was isn't there anymore."

Simon looked perplexed. "Huh. I figured it lived down there."

"Maybe it was a GHOST!" Jack said.

"There's no such thing as ghosts," Simon scoffed. "I told you that. Everybody be quiet for a minute and let's see if we hear it."

They all stopped talking and listened. All Henry

could hear was Jack's loud breathing, and a bird twittering far away. There was no sound coming from the cellar.

"Oh well," Simon said. "I guess it isn't there anymore. Let's see if we can find a way upstairs to the rooms. First we need the keys, in case they're locked. What were the room numbers, Delilah?"

Delilah fished a yellow Post-it note out of her shorts pocket. "Julia Thomas was in room six," she said. "The Petra . . . those German guys were in room five."

"The Petrasch brothers," Henry said.

Simon stepped carefully behind the high counter where rows of keys, brown with age, hung on a rack of hooks on the wall. "Here," he said triumphantly. "Five!" Then he paused. "Huh. Six isn't here." He scanned the rows of hooks. "Oh well, there are some missing. Maybe we'll be able to break in to the room without it."

"But how are we even going to get to the second floor?" Henry asked. "The bottom stairs are rotted away." Even if they could think of a way to climb past the first few rotten steps, he had no confidence that the upper stairs would be sturdy enough to walk on. He had visions of trying to get to the second floor and then plummeting twelve or fourteen feet through the air. What if they broke through the boards again and fell into the cellar?

"Let's look around," Simon said, shoving the key to room five in his pocket. "We didn't go into the saloon last time."

Henry saw that there were double doors on the other side of the hotel's lobby, with the remnants of colored glass windows inset into the upper panels. Shards of green and gold glass sparkled on the floor in front of them.

"Watch your step," Simon cautioned, leading the way.

They stepped over the broken glass and pushed through the doors, which creaked loudly on rusted hinges. Beyond the threshold was a large room with a few broken chairs scattered around and a three-legged table in the center. Shafts of sun shone through the dusty windows, barely illuminating its contours. There was a long, high bar on one side. Behind the bar were rows of shelves, with broken glass covering them. There must have been a mirror back there, Henry realized. This was the bar where people sat to order drinks. He tried to picture the room in its heyday, crowded with cowboys and miners drinking whiskey and listening to music.

"Wow! What kind of place is this?" Delilah said, gazing around. "Look at the old furniture. . . . And do you see the stuff on the walls?"

"This is the place where everyone came to have fun," Henry said, trying to think of an interesting-sounding word from all the books he had read that might describe it. "It must have been very . . . *festive* here."

"What's that mean?" Jack demanded.

"A place that would be perfect for parties."

In the dim light, Henry could make out a couple of light fixtures and some framed pictures on the wall. He walked over to one of them, a vertical rectangle slightly bigger than a magazine. It was a faded ink drawing of the hotel, with its sign hanging over the door and the black cat clearly visible. The picture frame was cracked, the glass broken.

"They're drawings," he said. "This one's of the hotel. The one next to it . . ." He peered at it more closely. "It looks like the town. We saw this church, remember? With the steeple?" He touched his fingertip lightly to the picture.

Simon came over to stand beside him. "Yeah, that's right. It's the church at the end of the street. So this is what Gold Creek looked like back when people lived here! That means these are a hundred years old." He sighed. "It's too bad they're in such bad shape."

Henry looked around the room. There were several

more pictures, but they were all badly damaged, the paper discolored and torn, the ink so faded it was difficult to see what they depicted.

"Here's a picture of some guy," Delilah offered. She pointed to what appeared to be a portrait of a man in an old-fashioned suit, with a thick handlebar mustache.

"I wonder who that is," Henry said.

"Hey," Jack called. He was poking around behind the bar. "There are stairs over here! In the corner. And they're not broken!"

"I thought so!" Simon said jubilantly. "Let's find Julia Thomas's room."

Jack started to bound up the stairs, but Henry grabbed his shirt. "Go slowly! Just in case."

They climbed the dark stairs and stepped onto the landing of an even darker hallway. It was lined with closed doors.

"Do they still have the numbers on them?" Delilah asked.

Simon shook his head. "Not all of them. But some do. Here, this is room three." Simon pointed to a faded number painted high in the center of one of the doors. He tried the door handle, and it turned but the door stayed shut. "I don't think they're locked. Just stuck."

He leaned his shoulder against the door and pushed. It squeaked in protest, then popped open.

They all crowded into the doorway. There were two windows overlooking the street, the glass in several panes broken, and paint peeled in large flakes off the walls. A thin, stained mattress lay in the corner, and a big, splintering wardrobe stood against the wall. Otherwise, the room was empty.

"We should make sure there's nothing inside here," Delilah said, crossing the room to the wardrobe. She pulled on one of the knobs, then pulled harder. The door swung partway open and ground to a halt on the warped frame.

She peered inside. "Nothing," she said in disappointment.

"Okay, let's find rooms five and six and see if there's anything in them. Then we can check the others," Simon decided. He turned on the flashlight and shone it along the hallway, at the twin rows of closed doors.

It was both quieter and darker up here than downstairs. Henry felt a thin prick of foreboding.

But Jack walked fearlessly down the hallway. "This is four. This is five. This doesn't have a number," he announced, poking his finger at the last door on the left side of the hall.

"Then maybe that's six, Julia Thomas's room," Delilah said.

Simon was already turning the door handle of room five and forcing his way inside. Henry, Jack, and Delilah crowded after him. The room had only a small window and was bare except for an empty glass bottle on the floor, thickly covered in dust, and a chair leaning against one wall. Its wooden seat was split down the middle.

"Shine the flashlight on the floor," Henry suggested, "in case there's something there."

Simon waved the flashlight back and forth, casting light into the corners of the room. Besides the bottle, there wasn't so much as a penny.

"There's NOTHING up here," Jack said dejectedly.

"I wonder why the librarian and Officer Myers and Sara Delgado's dad were talking about it, then," Henry said. "Why did they think there would be something at the hotel?"

"Probably the same reason we did," Simon said. "Because Julia Thomas stayed here with the Petrasch brothers both before and *after* they climbed the mountain looking for the gold."

"But they wouldn't have left the gold here if they found any," Henry pointed out.

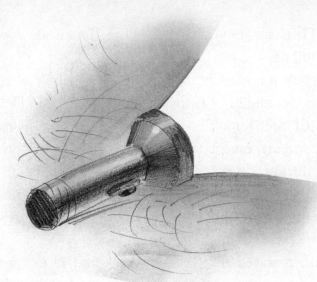

"No," Simon agreed, "but they might have left something else, something from their trip that would tell us if they *did* find gold, and where it might be."

"Well, they don't seem to have left anything," Henry argued. "And this place gives me a bad feeling. I think we should go."

"Okay, okay, but we have to check out room six," Simon said.

"Yeah, Henry," Jack said reprovingly. "Don't be a baby."

"If we all stick together, nothing bad will happen," Delilah said. Henry wondered about her reasoning on this, since they had all been together when Delilah fell down the side of the canyon and when the avalanche happened. But before he had time to point that out, they were standing in room six, Julia Thomas's room.

It was the corner room, with windows overlooking both the main street through Gold Creek and the rolling desert, their panes clouded and cracked. The room was completely empty, except for another large, battered wardrobe.

Delilah walked over to the wardrobe, yanking it open, her braid swinging.

"Anything?" Simon asked.

"Nope," she said. "I guess it makes sense that there wouldn't be anything valuable, you know? Somebody would have found it by now."

"Yeah," Simon agreed, swinging the flashlight in a wide arc, lighting the room's walls and floor.

"Wait," said Henry. "What's that?"

On the wall between the two windows that over-looked the desert was a framed picture.

"It's another one of those drawings," Delilah said, following Henry toward the spot where it hung.

Together, they leaned toward the picture, which appeared to be of a woman. "Simon," Henry began, "shine the light—"

But Simon had already directed the flashlight's beam to the picture.

Delilah gasped. "Hey! It's a picture of Julia Thomas, and she's holding a cat. . . ."

Jack ran over to them. "A black cat!" he cried.

Henry stood frozen, staring at the picture. The paper was frayed and stained, but he could see that it was an ink drawing of Julia Thomas, immediately recognizable, the eerie twin of the librarian, with her wings of dark hair and high cheekbones. She was sitting upright in a high-backed chair. On her lap, inside the curve of her arm, was a black cat.

A cat with a white splotch on its neck.

A cat that looked exactly like Josie.

CHAPTER 6
NOT ALONE

"HEY," JACK SAID. "Doesn't that cat look like . . . ?" He turned to Henry uncertainly.

Simon was standing with them now, shining the flashlight directly on the picture, the beam reflecting off the cracked glass. "That's weird," he said.

"It's Josie," Henry said quietly. "Look at the mark on her neck."

"Of course it isn't Josie," Simon snapped. He pulled up the hem of his T-shirt and rubbed the glass. "But it sure does look like her," he admitted.

Delilah leaned close to the picture, her brow furrowed. "Even the expression looks like Josie. Do you remember reading anything about Julia Thomas having a cat?" she asked Henry.

Henry shook his head. "No . . . but there wasn't much

about Julia Thomas in those books from the library." He continued to stare at the picture.

"I don't think the cat on the hotel sign has a spot on its neck," Simon said.

"We just couldn't see it," Henry said. "The sign is too faded."

"Well, at least this seems like the right room," Simon said. "Why would they have her picture hanging in here unless she stayed here?"

"Why would they have her picture hanging here . . . even if she did stay here?" Henry asked. "It's not like she was famous or something."

"Maybe she was more famous than we thought," Delilah offered.

"Or her cat was," Jack added.

"Let's take it with us," Simon said. "It's hard to really see it with only the flashlight."

Henry bit his lip. "Do you think that's okay? It's not ours."

But Simon was already lifting the picture carefully off the wall. "It's not anybody's now," he said. "The town was abandoned. It's the same as people leaving stuff out by the curb for the garbage man."

It didn't quite seem the same as that to Henry. But he

was anxious to leave the hotel, so he said nothing as Simon tucked the picture under one arm and swung the flashlight back to the hallway.

"Let's have a quick look in the other rooms, then we'll go," he said.

They opened the doors on the other side of the hallway and quickly checked those rooms. There was another old mattress, a broken table, and part of a wooden headboard in one. But the rest were empty, and there were no more pictures on the walls.

The boys and Delilah carefully descended the stairs

and were retracing their steps through the saloon when Henry heard something.

"Simon, wait," he said. "Be quiet for a minute."

It was a rustling sound, fast and hushed, a steady shifting murmur below their feet.

Simon turned slowly toward Henry, his eyes wide. "It's coming from the cellar," he said.

"Let's get out of here," Delilah said, starting past them into the hotel lobby.

"Stay near the wall," Simon warned her. He had his flashlight ready, shining the light over the floorboards and into the gaping hole, where the persistent soft scrabbling was growing louder.

Henry wanted nothing more than to flee into the bright sunshine of the street. But for once, the need to know what was beneath them outpaced his fear. The instinct to look was stronger than the instinct to run.

With his breath caught in his throat, Henry pressed shoulder to shoulder with Simon, leaning toward the broken edge of blackness, his eyes following the beam of the flashlight.

"AHHH!" Simon yelped, jumping backward and almost knocking Henry to the floor.

Down in the cellar, crawling over the pile of sacks in a slithering swarm were rats . . . a dark moving mound of rats. Their sleek humped backs and long tails blended and separated as they scavenged for crumbs. As the children watched in horror, a sharp nose and bright beady eyes turned upward toward them. The rustling continued, the rats scouring the burlap surface for the last remnants of granola.

"Ewwww! YUCK!" Jack cried. "Simon, those were down there with you! What if they had bitten you? What if they had gobbled you up?"

"Shut up, Jack," Simon said, but his face was pale. "Let's get out of here!"

Delilah, who'd been silent, was backing toward the door.

Simon tossed Henry the flashlight so he could grab the strap of his backpack. They all ran, no longer even bothering to watch where they stepped. In seconds, they were thumping onto the sagging porch, then down the splintered steps. There were the bikes, flashing colorfully in the bright sunlight.

Simon had the picture of Julia Thomas wedged under his arm. "Try to fit it in my backpack," he told Henry, sliding the straps over his shoulder and turning around.

Henry shifted the water bottles. "There's too much other stuff in here," he said. "There isn't room."

"Here," Delilah said, taking the water bottles. "We can put these and the flashlight in my bike basket." Henry thought, not for the first time, that Delilah was a useful sort of person, especially for a girl. He emptied Simon's backpack and gently slid the picture inside. Then he pulled the zipper up as far as he could to hold it in place.

With Henry toting the flashlight, Delilah holding the water bottles, and Jack carrying the granola bars, they clambered onto their bikes.

"Look," Jack said as he steered into the dusty street. "There's a car coming."

He pointed down the wagon trail toward the road. Henry shielded his eyes with his hand and squinted into the white summer light. A car had just turned off the road and was heading toward them, its tires churning up great clouds of brown dust.

"What would a car be doing out here?" he asked.

"You guys . . ." Delilah stopped, her brow creased. "That's a police car."

Henry gasped. She was right. Across the top of the car, he could just barely make out the rectangular bar of lights. He turned to her in a panic. "What if it's Officer Myers?"

"Let's go!" Simon said in a low voice. "Not down the path. Come on—behind the building. We'll have to ride through the field and hope he doesn't see us."

Quickly, they piled the water bottles, flashlight, and granola bars into Delilah's wicker basket and rolled their bikes around the corner of the hotel and into the desert, all the while watching the police car as it rolled steadily toward them. Simon steered his way through the brush and then climbed onto his bike and started pedaling, forging a trail. They rode behind the water tower and the church. If the rutted path had seemed challenging, the open field of shrubs, cactuses, and boulders was a veritable obstacle course, sandy dirt pushing against the bikes' tires. Henry realized that Simon was trying to navigate behind a screen of larger bushes and saguaros, but the rough terrain meant he kept having to stop and change direction, struggling to turn his front wheel in the resistant sand. Jack fell off twice, the second time crashing into a large rock. But even he understood the need to keep quiet. Henry felt a pang of sympathy when he saw that the rosy scrape on Jack's knee was starting to seep blood.

Meanwhile, they could see the police car rumbling up the dirt trail to the ghost town in a swirling cloud of dust.

When they finally made it back to the road, Simon began pedaling even faster.

"Can we slow down now?" Jack whined. "My knee hurts. It's BLEEDING."

"No," Simon said. "Don't stop."

"But—" Jack started to protest.

"We'll put a Band-Aid on it," Delilah told him. "But we have to get to your house first."

"Do you think he's following us?" Henry asked, struggling to keep up.

"He might if he sees our bike tracks," Simon said.

Delilah glanced over her shoulder. "Look, he stopped the car. He's probably poking around."

Henry felt a wave of relief. He tried to think if they'd left any sign that they'd been there. "We took everything with us, didn't we?"

"Sure," Simon said. "Oops! Even the room key." He pulled the rusty brown key to room five out of his pocket and turned it over in his palm.

Henry stiffened. "You took that?"

"It doesn't matter," Simon reasoned. "The doors weren't locked, and there were other keys missing." Then he added apologetically, "I forgot to put it back after we looked in the cellar. . . ."

Henry shuddered, thinking of the black cellar and the slithering blanket of rats. Weeks ago, when Simon fell through the floorboards, who could have known that's what was down there? He thought of the granola bar they'd dropped into the cellar. That was something they'd left behind . . . but surely it had been devoured by now.

Still marveling over their discoveries in the ghost town, they rode the rest of the way home.

CHAPTER 7
PAST LIVES

THE NEXT MORNING, Henry woke up early, after a night full of terrible dreams. He couldn't remember all of them, but the last one, the one that had awakened him bolt upright, with his heart seized in terror, was this: Josie had followed the boys to the ghost town, and before they could stop her she leapt into the cellar of the Black Cat Saloon. At first she was chasing the rats, but then they turned on her, swarming around her. The boys were desperately trying to get her out, reaching as far as they could into the hole and calling to her, and she looked like she was just about to jump into Henry's arms when out of nowhere, the librarian Julia Thomas came into the hotel and also leaned over the hole. When Josie saw the librarian, her back arched and she yowled in fury, just the way she had outside the meeting of the historical society. But then as the rats surrounded Josie, getting closer and closer with their twitching noses and plump haunches and sharp teeth, the old Julia Thomas, the one from the picture, emerged from a dark corner of the cellar and held out her arms. Josie leapt into them, and the old Julia Thomas clutched her against her old-fashioned, high-buttoned dress, and disappeared back into the darkness. In the dream, Henry was leaning so far into the cellar he thought he might fall, screaming "Josie! Josie!" But she was gone. All he could see were the rats.

Heart pounding, Henry slid out of bed and wandered down the quiet hallway toward the kitchen. Josie lay in the doorway in a pale rectangle of morning light, watching him with her golden eyes. Henry felt a rush of love and relief. He knelt on the carpet and stroked her silky head, scratching behind her ears. She leaned into his fingers, curving her neck, and he could feel more than hear the warm, humming motor of her purring. Then, abruptly, her ears flattened and she rolled onto her back, batting his hand with her paws.

"Okay, okay," Henry said, trying to scratch her soft belly, just below the patch of white. But Josie leapt up and darted into the living room, finished with him.

He thought about the old ink picture of Julia Thomas

with the cat on her lap. It looked so much like Josie! Right down to the distinctive white spot on her neck. How was that possible?

"Is that you, Henry?" Mrs. Barker's voice drifted through the open door of her study. "You're up early."

"Yeah. I had a bad dream." Henry walked over to her drafting table, rubbing his eyes. She was already hard at work, carefully sketching the contours of a heart with thick, bulging arteries. Her latest project was a series of illustrations for a book on heart disease.

Mrs. Barker slid her arm around him and pulled him against her, kissing his shoulder. "What was the dream about?"

He frowned, not sure how much to tell her. "I can't remember all of it. Something bad happened to Josie."

"Oh, that must have been scary! Well, she's lying there in the hallway. Did you see her?"

He nodded, leaning against his mother's warm body, watching her draw. There was something soothing about the way her hand moved over the paper, so deftly, with such certainty. It gave him a hypnotic, tingly feeling, like having somebody stroke his hair.

"What's wrong with that heart?" Henry asked. It was strange to him, knowing nothing about what a heart looked like, that he could still know instantly there was something wrong with the one his mother was drawing. The tubes running through it were bloated and thick. They looked ready to explode.

"It's a condition called atherosclerosis," his mother answered. "Thickening of the arteries. It can cause a heart attack."

"Atherosclerosis," Henry repeated, liking the long, round sound of the word.

His mother kept drawing, and the poor, diseased heart took shape under her hand.

"Mom," he said after a minute.

"What, honey?"

"Do you think it's possible for somebody who lived a long time ago to come back to life? In another person?"

"No," his mother answered.

Somehow this wasn't quite what Henry was looking for. "Not ever?"

"No, sweetie. Not ever. Death doesn't work that way." He waited for her to say more, but she continued drawing, absorbed in the picture taking shape on the page. "Why do you ask?"

"I was just thinking about it," he said slowly. "We

saw a picture. . . ." He tried to think of a way to tell her and not tell her at the same time. "It was in a book at the library—a picture of that woman Julia Thomas, the one whose grave Emmett found when he went to Phoenix. She lived here in the 1800s. . . ."

"Mmm-hmmm," his mother murmured, intent on her work.

"Mom." Henry touched her shoulder, wanting her to pay attention. A flash of irritation crossed her face, but she stopped drawing, balancing the pencil in her hand. "What is it, Hen? What are you worried about?"

"The Julia Thomas in the book, who lived in the 1800s, has the same name as the lady who works at the library . . . and looks just like her!"

At that moment, Mr. Barker leaned in the doorway, a steaming cup of coffee in his hand. "That woman at the library? I didn't care for her. You're telling me there was another one of her, a hundred years ago? Isn't that the way it always is! The people you'd like to have reincarnated are gone for good, but the rotten ones keep coming back like a bad penny."

Mrs. Barker laughed but shook her head at him. "Don't give Henry ideas."

"What does that mean?" Henry asked. "*Reincarnated?*"

Mrs. Barker sighed. "Brought back to life in another form. Reincarnation is the belief, in some religions, that when people die, they can return to life. In the form of other people or animals."

"Really?" Henry looked at his father. "Do you think that can happen?"

"No," Mrs. Barker interjected firmly.

Mr. Barker sipped his coffee. "Well, I don't know, Hen . . . the world is a complicated place, and different religions for many centuries have had the belief in reincarnation. Hinduism, some parts of Judaism, Native American religions . . ." His eyes sparkled, warming up to the idea. "Now, isn't it interesting that all those different religions, from all over the world, have a common belief in past lives? In the possibility of the dead returning, as a new person, or as an animal? Okay, maybe it's a little wacky, but I've got to say, I think there's a lot we don't know about death."

Mrs. Barker put down her pencil and turned away from the drafting table to look at him, her mouth set in an impatient line. "Jim."

He laughed at her. "Oh well, you heard your mother." He picked up the empty mug on her desk. "More coffee?"

"Yes, thanks," she said, slightly mollified. She returned to work, while Henry trailed his father into the kitchen.

"So you think people can be reincarnated? What about animals?" he asked.

"I don't know, Henry. But if people can come back from the dead, I don't see why animals wouldn't be able to."

"Dad," Henry began, carefully, "the other thing about this picture of the old Julia Thomas, the one from the 1800s, is that she had a cat. A cat that looked just like Josie, Dad! With the white mark and everything—the one on her neck that's shaped like Florida."

His father laughed. "Is it shaped like Florida? I've never noticed that."

Henry slumped into a kitchen chair, ready to give up. It seemed impossible to make either of his parents understand.

His father refilled the mug for his mother and then walked over to the table, ruffling Henry's curls. "What's the matter, Hen? Why all this interest in reincarnation?"

Henry shook off his hand in exasperation. "Because the woman in the old picture, the woman who lived in the 1800s, looked just like the librarian! And her cat looked just like Josie!"

Mr. Barker studied him. "Okay, okay. That *is* weird. You'll have to show me the picture—now I want to see it for myself."

Henry squirmed. This was exactly why Simon would have told him not to say a thing. He tried one last time. "Do you think Josie could be a reincarnated cat from the 1800s? Who used to live right here in Superstition?"

Mr. Barker appeared to consider this. "Well, they do say cats have nine lives," he offered cheerfully. "And Josie certainly seems to feel at home here in Arizona. Speak of the devil, here she is."

Josie padded softly into the kitchen, then jumped onto the table—where she was never, ever allowed—to sniff the placemats. Mr. Barker ran his hand down her back, and winked at Henry. "Shhhh, don't tell your mother."

"Why do you think Mom doesn't believe in reincarnation?"

"Well . . . your mother has a particular kind of imagination," Mr. Barker declared philosophically. "A wonderful head for knowledge, but no sense of the mythical." He headed down the hallway with her mug of coffee.

Henry was left face-to-face with Josie, who crossed

the table till her nose was almost touching his and stared at him with her golden eyes. Had she really once belonged to the old Julia Thomas? Had she lived in the shadow of Superstition Mountain more than a century ago? It might explain why she was so comfortable in the cemetery . . . and why she seemed to just *know* things that none of the rest of them did.

CHAPTER 8
HIDDEN PICTURES

BY THE TIME his brothers woke up, Henry could hardly wait to look at the picture from the hotel again. All he could think about was the image of the cat nestled on Julia Thomas's lap, and how much it looked like Josie. While Simon and Jack were sleeping, he had called Delilah twice, only to be told by her mother—first patiently and then with a hint of annoyance—that she too was still asleep. Finally, everyone was awake, and Delilah immediately came over on her bike, with her hair still in a messy braid from the day before.

She joined Simon and Jack at the kitchen table for breakfast, while Henry told them all about reincarnation. Unfortunately, Mr. Barker wasn't around to lend supporting evidence; he had already left for work at his masonry shop in town, where he mixed concrete for sidewalks and patio paving stones. But at least Mrs. Barker was so absorbed in her sketches that she didn't pepper the discussion with skeptical remarks.

Simon, as it turned out, already knew about reincarnation. "But I don't think that's what people mean when they say a cat has nine lives," he said. "I think it means that they don't die easily."

Henry thought about this. "Well, it could mean both—they don't die easily, and when they do, they come back for another life."

"Cool!" Jack exclaimed. "So you think Josie is a GHOST cat? She lived a long, long time ago?" He ducked under the table, where Josie had fled when he stampeded into the kitchen minutes earlier, and scooped her up in his arms. "Are you a GHOST, Josie?" he yelled into her face. "Are you?"

Josie shrank back in disgust and squirmed, pressing both paws against his chest until she leveraged herself free. She leapt through the air to the floor and streaked off.

"She hates it when you do that," Henry said mildly.

"Yeah, 'cuz she's a GHOST!" Jack exclaimed. "Ghosts don't like to be touched."

"Boys," Mrs. Barker called from her study, "what are you yelling about?"

Simon glared at Jack. "Nothing, Mom. Jack is just goofing around."

Delilah seemed lost in thought. "I didn't think reincarnation meant that you came back as *yourself.* I thought it meant you came back as somebody else. Or as something else, like a person coming back as an animal." She hesitated. "I used to wish my dad would be reincarnated as something. Since we moved out here, there's been this hummingbird . . ." Her voice trailed off.

"What?" Henry asked. He loved hummingbirds, with their tiny faces and their shimmering colors and their wings that beat a thousand times a minute. It always seemed impossible that they were real.

Delilah looked at the floor. "I don't know. It comes to the feeder on our deck every single day, and sometimes it stays in front of the sliding glass doors with its wings beating and just watches us. It makes me think of my dad."

Simon seemed about to say something dismissive, but then he looked at Delilah and, to Henry's surprise, said only, "Well, lots of religions do believe in reincarnation." Delilah shot him a grateful glance, and Henry wished he had been the one to say that.

"I think hummingbirds are . . . *exquisite,*" he chimed in.

Delilah laughed. "You know so many funny words, Henry."

It wasn't quite the response he had hoped for. "Where did you put the picture?" he asked Simon, wanting to change the subject. "Let's look at it again."

"It's still in my backpack." Simon led the way to his bedroom and knelt next to his bed, pulling his backpack out from underneath it. The wooden frame of the picture burst through the open zipper. Carefully, he slid it out of the backpack and set it down on the carpet. "Close the door," he told Jack.

Jack shut the bedroom door and they all dropped to the carpet, leaning over the pen-and-ink drawing. It was faded and stained, but the image of Julia Thomas was unmistakable. . . . Her dark hair fell neatly from a center part, gathered into a bun at her neck. Her eyebrows were thin and arched, just like the librarian's, and her eyes had a burning intensity. On her lap was the cat, sitting upright in the curve of her arm. Its ears were pricked and its light eyes gazed impassively out of the picture. The white spot on its neck had the familiar dangling-sock shape of Josie's.

"Yep," Jack declared. "It's Josie."

Simon rolled his eyes. "Do you know how common black cats are? Even black cats with white spots!"

"But, Simon . . ." Henry hesitated. "It's not just the coloring. Look at the cat's expression! It's exactly like Josie's."

"So what are you saying, Hen? You think Josie lived here a hundred and thirty years ago? And then died and came back to life as our pet? Seriously?"

Henry sighed. "I don't know. But it would explain a lot, don't you think? How Josie seems to know her way around out here, even on the mountain. How she finds things, like that tombstone in the graveyard that had our name on it, or that piece of Uncle Hank's stationery in the gold mine."

Simon pursed his lips in exasperation. "It would make more sense to say that she's related to Julia Thomas's cat— that that cat was her distant ancestor. But I still wouldn't believe it. The cat in this picture must have lived in Arizona more than a hundred years ago. Mom and Dad got Josie from a shelter in Chicago."

Henry shook his head. "If Josie were just related to the black cat from the saloon, the way we're related to Uncle Hank, that wouldn't explain how she knows so much about this place. And it wouldn't explain the weird reaction she had to the librarian."

Simon paused. "But think about that, Hen. If Josie were really Julia Thomas's cat, and the librarian is so similar to the first Julia Thomas, why would Josie have acted so upset when she saw her?"

Henry couldn't think of a good answer to that.

"Well, Henry's right about one thing," Delilah interjected. "This cat looks exactly like Josie. I wonder who drew the picture—it isn't signed. Do you think it says on the back?"

Gently, she turned the picture over on the carpeting. The back of it was a thin piece of wood, which must have been what the paper was mounted on, Henry decided.

"Can we take this off and look?" Delilah asked. "Without wrecking the picture?"

"Let's try," Simon said. "The frame is broken anyway." He carefully pulled the sides of the frame away from the picture, loosening the piece of wood until he could remove it. "There," he said. "Did the artist sign it?"

He set the piece of wood aside and they all stared. Underneath it, pressed against the back of the drawing, was a small, folded piece of ivory-colored stationery.

"Hey, there's something here. A note or something," Simon said slowly. He lifted it and pinched it open with his fingers.

"What does it say?" Jack cried, bouncing forward on his knees. "Read it to us!"

Simon's eyes widened as he read aloud: "*The canyon entrance is on the eastern wall, behind a group of large boulders. Two cottonwood trees grow opposite the boulders. The entrance is narrow, no wider than a man's shoulders. Continue toward the horse until the bent tree threads the needle.*"

"Those are the directions to the gold mine!" Jack yelled.

"Shhh, Jack," Simon hushed him. "But yeah, these are the same directions . . . and look! There's a map too." He turned the note for them to see a small, simple map sketched beneath the instructions. Squinting at it, Henry could see that it showed the little secret canyon with the rock horse and entrance to the mine. Above the map, several lines of crisp ink handwriting crossed the paper, delicate and slanting.

"Well, that would have been a big help," Jack said in exasperation. "Look, it shows the rock horse and everything. It would have been easy-peasy to find the mine if we'd had that."

"That handwriting," Delilah said, her brows furrowing. "It looks kind of familiar. Is it the same as the writing that's on the other note?"

"I don't think so," Henry said. He thought back to the day in the canyon, when they'd been searching for

the mine; how many times he'd read and reread the directions on the little scrap of paper they'd found in the secret compartment of Uncle Hank's coin box. The handwriting on this paper looked different, but—Delilah was right—also vaguely familiar.

"Somebody probably copied it," Simon said. "But let's compare them to make sure. You put that other note back in the coin box, didn't you, Hen?"

Henry nodded. Though it had only been a few weeks, it seemed so long ago that they had discovered the gold mine, returning home with the note of directions and

Jack's fistful of tiny gold flakes. "But why would the directions to the gold mine be here, behind the picture of Julia Thomas?"

"I don't know," Simon said. "And look—there's nothing on the back of the drawing itself. Nobody signed it or wrote on it."

"I wonder who made this picture," Delilah said softly. "And who hid the directions there."

"Yeah," Simon said. "It's kind of hard to tell if they did or didn't want them to be found. I mean, this *is* a picture of Julia Thomas, and she was the one Jacob Waltz told about the gold mine before he died."

Simon handed the note to Delilah, then quickly reassembled the picture and tucked it into his backpack, stashing it under the bed.

"Let's go downstairs to Uncle Hank's desk and look at the handwriting on that other piece of paper," he said.

CHAPTER 9
KEY TO THE PAST

MRS. BARKER EMERGED from her study just as they started down the hallway. "Delilah," she said, smiling. "I thought I heard your voice."

"Hi, Mrs. Barker," Delilah said. "Is it okay that I came over this early?"

"Of course," Mrs. Barker said. "You're always welcome here. In fact, I've been meaning to ask you and your mother to come over for a cookout one night. Maybe this evening? With Emmett and Kathy, while she's visiting. Do you know if you have plans?"

"No, I don't think so—that would be great!"

"Well, we should call your mother to make sure. What are you four up to so early this morning?"

They looked at each other uncertainly. "We were just

going to have another look at Uncle Hank's coin collection," Simon said. "Downstairs in the desk. Is that okay?"

"Sure. I need to clean that out at some point." Mrs. Barker continued into the kitchen with her coffee mug, and Simon, Henry, Jack, and Delilah headed straight for the basement door.

Uncle Hank's old rolltop desk stood in a corner of the basement, its various contents consolidated by Mrs. Barker's post-move cleaning and organizing spree into just two of the large drawers. The coin box with the secret compartment that housed the directions to the gold mine was in the second drawer. Delilah gently unfolded the note that had been tucked inside the picture frame and set it on the desk. Simon pulled out the rusty-orange oblong box and slid open its concealed lower drawer, taking out the piece of torn, yellowed paper with the directions written on it. He flattened it next to the note from the picture and switched on the desk lamp. In the round glow of light, Henry could see that the handwriting was nothing alike.

Delilah sighed in disappointment. "It's not the same," she said.

"No," Simon agreed. "It's not even close. This

handwriting from the picture is so neat and small. And it's in real ink, not ballpoint pen."

"Why does it look familiar?" Delilah puzzled. "I could swear I've seen it before." She picked up the ivory note and squinted at it.

"Wait," Henry said, staring at the slanting black lines of script. "It's . . . it's the same as the handwriting in the hotel ledger!" He turned excitedly to Delilah. "Isn't it?"

"Yes," she cried. "That's it! It's Julia Thomas's handwriting. That's why I recognized it. But what does that mean?"

"It means that Julia Thomas herself wrote the directions and drew the map!" Simon said jubilantly. "And that makes sense. Remember? Emmett said that when she couldn't find the gold mine herself on that trip up the mountain with the German brothers, she drew maps showing where it might be, based on Jacob Waltz's instructions, and started selling them to people. So maybe this is just one of the maps, with directions. And someone stuck it behind her picture in the hotel."

Jack picked up the torn scrap of paper from the coin box. "But what about these directions? Who wrote these?"

They all considered the note silently. "Someone must

have copied the original directions and given them to Uncle Hank," Henry said. "But who?"

"Not Julia Thomas the librarian," Delilah said thoughtfully. "'Cuz we know her handwriting looks exactly like the handwriting of the first Julia Thomas. I almost wish I was still wearing my cast so we could compare them, side by side."

"Right," Simon said. "It was somebody else. Not Uncle Hank, not either of the Julia Thomases. Somebody who was helping Uncle Hank look for the gold mine?"

Henry pulled the drawer all the way open, propping it with his knee so it wouldn't tumble onto the floor. "What about all these letters and cards?" he said. "We haven't looked through any of these yet." He lifted the stack of postcards and letters tied together with string that they had found at the beginning of the summer, when they first explored Uncle Hank's desk. Henry had noticed them before but hadn't thought there was anything special about them. Now it seemed like they could be the key to figuring out who was the author of the note in the coin box.

"That's a great idea, Hen," Simon said enthusiastically, and as always when Simon praised him, Henry felt his heart swell with pride. It almost meant more to him than having his parents compliment him, because Simon's praise was so rare, and much harder to earn. Also, he knew that Simon never said nice things to encourage him or because his spirits needed boosting.

Henry couldn't get the string unknotted with his stubby nails, so Delilah took over. After a minute or two, she untied it, and was starting to fan out the letters and cards so they could look at them when something fell heavily out of the packet and thumped onto the carpet.

"What's that?" Jack asked, reaching for it.

But Simon grabbed it first. "Hey . . . ," he said. He held it aloft.

It was a rusty metal key. Simon fished in his pocket

and held up the key to room five that he had brought back from the ghost town.

Henry saw that the two keys looked identical. He gasped.

"It must be the key to room six! The key to the room Julia Thomas stayed in!"

CHAPTER 10
A PERFECT MATCH

"DO YOU KNOW what this means?" Simon asked, his voice breathless.

Delilah leaned forward on her knees and scattered the postcards and letters in a wave of enthusiastic confetti over the carpet. "It means your Uncle Hank went to the Black Cat Hotel and Saloon! And he took the key to Julia Thomas's room."

"Or somebody gave it to him," Henry said. "Why was the key in that batch of letters? Maybe it fell out of one of them."

Simon ran his hand over his spiky hair, making it stand on end. "Either way, he had the key," he said. "So it's safe to assume he was in her hotel room."

"Do you think he found anything there?" Jack asked eagerly. "Maybe he found the GOLD!"

"Maybe." Simon continued to rub his hair, frowning slightly. "But those rooms were pretty cleaned out."

"Let's look through these cards and letters," Delilah suggested. "We can see if there's handwriting that matches the note from the coin box, and maybe we'll be able to tell if the key came from a letter that's here."

"Okay," Simon directed. "Look for handwriting that matches this." He waved the scrap of paper from the coin box under their noses.

"You are always making us READ things," Jack complained. "And I can't read. It's no fair."

"You'll learn to read this year, in first grade," Henry told him. "And you know all the letters. You don't have to be able to read to match the handwriting—just compare the letters, like the capital *C* and the *V*'s, or how the *A*'s look."

"Yeah," Delilah added. "Pretend you're a detective. It's like trying to figure out if two drawings are by the same artist."

"Pretend you're Encyclopedia Brown," Henry encouraged him. "Remember how I read those books to you, and we were always trying to figure out the clues? This is something Encyclopedia Brown would do."

Jack's grumpy expression softened. "Okay," he conceded. "I'm a good detective."

Simon put the two keys on top of the desk. Crouched in a ring on the carpet, they began sifting through the pile of correspondence. There were postcards from various friends of Uncle Hank's, with colorful pictures of white beaches and old churches and nighttime cityscapes. When Henry turned them over, he saw cheery scribbled messages from these far-flung locales. He found a postcard all the way from Australia—Australia!—and one from Las Vegas, with a neon-lit casino on it. There were even a few postcards from the Barker family on their various vacations. It was funny to read affectionate messages from Mr. Barker to Uncle Hank that had been written years ago, some of them before Jack was even born. It seemed strange to Henry that the letters still existed, when Uncle Hank no longer did. He saw his father's jagged scrawl and tried to picture him in that moment, a young dad with babies, writing to his beloved uncle.

"Listen to this," Henry said, lifting a postcard that Mr. Barker had sent to Uncle Hank from their family camping trip to Yellowstone National Park. "*Yellowstone is spectacular—saw the hot springs yesterday. Also, lots of buffalo. We'll have to come back when the kids are older. Camping with diapers is not as fun! Love, Jim and the gang."*

"I remember that trip!" Simon grinned. "We saw bears."

"BEARS!" Jack protested. "Was I there too? I never saw a bear."

"Well, you were a baby," Henry told him. "Look at the date—you were two. I can barely remember it." He had only the vaguest recollection of a green tent in a forested campsite, and his father lifting him high above a wooden railing to see the steaming turquoise waters of the hot springs. But now he wondered if he really remembered it, or if he'd just seen pictures of the trip and was remembering those. It was so long ago.

"It's not fair," Jack grumbled. "You got to see BEARS."

"You saw them too," Simon told him. "It's not our fault you don't remember."

Jack's face clouded, and Henry could see him balling up a fist, ready to slug Simon.

He tried to intercede. "Hey—"

But Delilah came to the rescue. "You guys," she said. "Look." She was holding a folded blue note card in one hand and the torn scrap of the gold-mine directions in the other. "I found it!"

Henry felt his heart quicken. He could see that the generous, rounded letters on the blue card matched the ones on the paper. "It's the same handwriting! Who's it from?"

"There are initials on the front," Delilah said, showing them the letters *PAC* engraved in navy. The *A* was larger than the other two letters, a formidable triangle centered between them.

"It's a *monogram*," Henry corrected her.

Simon added, "The *A* is the biggest, so it's from somebody with a first name that starts with *P* and a last name that starts with *A*."

But Delilah had opened the card and was lost in its message. "Wow," she said slowly.

"What is it?" Simon demanded. "What does it say?"

"It's . . ." Her eyes were riveted on the blue paper.

"Come on," Jack demanded. "Read it!"

Delilah looked at Henry, her brows drawn together. "I don't know. It seems . . . private."

Simon shook his head impatiently. "Nothing is private after you're dead."

He reached out to take the blue note card from Delilah, but she held on to it. Henry wondered if that was true. Did you lose your privacy when you died? Did that mean it was okay for other people to find out all your secrets? It didn't seem quite right to him, but Simon said it with such certainty.

"No. I'll read it," Delilah said, tightening her grasp. She tossed her long braid over her shoulder and bowed her head, reading slowly: *"My love, I am sorry about today. I want you to find what you're looking for. Here's the key. You already have a more important one . . . the key to the chambers of my heart. I am yours always. Prita."*

CHAPTER 11
THE ONE

"YUCK," SAID JACK, wrinkling his nose. "That's too lovey-dovey."

"No it's not," Delilah answered staunchly. "I think it's beautiful."

"The key!" Henry said. "Not only is that the person who copied the directions to the gold mine . . . she gave Uncle Hank the key to room six!"

"Who is it again?" Simon took the note from Delilah. "*P-R-I-T-A* . . . Prita? Like Rita. Never heard of her. But I guess ol' Uncle Hank had a girlfriend."

"More than a girlfriend," Delilah contradicted. "A true love."

"You can't tell that from one letter," Simon told her.

"There's not just one," Delilah said. "Look." From

the scattered pile of postcards, she lifted a thick packet of identical blue cards, tied with a ribbon. Not a string, like the stack of correspondence; a pale sliver of white ribbon.

"*Love* letters?" Henry asked in amazement. "But Uncle Hank was supposed to be a player." It was the word his mother had used to describe Uncle Hank once, a word that—confusingly—meant something bad: a man who had a lot of girlfriends at the same time, or one girlfriend after another, with no long relationships. Henry had to agree with Delilah; the words on the blue note card did not sound like something a woman would write to a man who had other girlfriends.

"Let's read them," Simon said, stretching out his hand. But Delilah eluded him, snatching the stack of cards behind her back.

"No," she said firmly. "We shouldn't have read this one. They weren't meant for anyone but your uncle Hank."

"What are you talking about?" Simon glared at her. "You don't get to decide that."

Henry almost laughed, because it sounded so much like something Jack would say to Simon. And indeed, Jack immediately chimed in.

"Yeah! You are not the boss of us!"

Delilah was unfazed. "We should return them to this woman, Prita. That's the right thing to do."

"But they're Uncle Hank's letters!" Simon protested. "They belong to us now."

Henry considered this. Did letters get inherited like all the other stuff in their uncle's house? Or now that he was gone, did they belong to the person who wrote them?

"Okay," Delilah said coolly, springing to her feet. "Let's ask your mom what she thinks."

Simon groaned. "You're such a tattletale."

"Yeah!" Jack yelled. "TATTLETALE!"

"You said there was nothing wrong with reading the letters," Delilah retorted. "If that's true, why do you care if we ask your mom?"

"Well, geez, Delilah, you know our *mom* will see something wrong with it," Simon protested. "Moms are just like that."

As if on cue, Mrs. Barker's voice drifted down the basement stairs. "What's all the yelling about?"

Delilah stood poised, the packet of blue note cards clutched behind her back. She shot Simon a challenging glance.

He rolled his eyes in frustration. "Nothing, Mom," he called. "Jack and Delilah are just arguing about something."

Outraged, Jack gaped, but they could all hear that their mother was still hesitating at the top of the stairs.

"Jack," she called, "do you need to come up here for a little break?"

"No!" Jack cried. "I wasn't doing anything!"

"It's okay, Mom," Henry interjected. "We can work it out."

Their mother was a big fan of working it out. She much preferred for the boys to solve their own disagreements, even if they did so unfairly, than to be called upon to referee. Simon, Henry, and Jack had learned this the hard way; whenever they got into an argument over something, even when one of them was clearly and gallingly right, Mrs. Barker would send all parties to their rooms to cool off. Her familiar warning was, "Don't make me sort this out, or none of you will end up happy."

Mr. Barker, meanwhile, loved to referee . . . and the more trivial the disagreement, the better. He would decide, unilaterally, who should get the last cookie, who won the argument about best superhero, and who did the most impressive job on his weekend chores. If one of their games got out of hand, he would jump in with suggestions, rather than trying to break things up, the way their mother did. The last time they played shark attack, he even supported Jack's attempt to drag Simon across the carpet by his feet, since for the purposes of the game, Jack was the great white shark.

Unlike their mother, their father liked to listen to all sides first—the pettier the complaints and accusations, the more interested he became—and then render a final verdict, like a judge in a courtroom. The good thing about Mr. Barker was that he had grown up with brothers of his own, so he knew all about fighting and the importance of winning. The bad thing was that he was shockingly unpredictable, so you never knew in advance what he would decide. But at least he didn't play favorites.

"Yeah, we'll work it out," Jack said desperately, sending Simon a dark look.

"Okay, but no more yelling," Mrs. Barker warned. "Oh, and Delilah? Would you mind giving your mom a call and checking on dinner tonight? If you can come over, I'll ask Mr. Barker to pick up a couple of things on his way home."

"Sure," Delilah said politely. "I'll call her right now."

She clamped the ribbon-tied stack of blue note cards securely under her arm and walked over to the phone.

As soon as they heard Mrs. Barker's steps receding down the hallway, Delilah turned to Simon, who was fuming, and said, "I'll tell you what we can do. We'll find this woman Prita. Then we can give her back the letters and ask her about your uncle Hank . . . and the key, and the directions to the mine. Maybe she knows something about the candle box full of gold."

"That's a good idea," Henry said, though he realized that she was probably only suggesting it to distract them from the argument over reading the love letters.

Simon groaned. "How are we supposed to do that? We don't know where she lives."

"We can look her up in the phone book," Delilah answered calmly.

"Um, no, we can't. We don't know her last name."

"But we have her initials," Delilah said.

"Phone books don't list people by initials, you goof. And we don't even know if she lives around here."

"Yeah, that's just DUMB," Jack added.

Henry thought for a minute. "We could ask Emmett. He seems to know a lot of people. And Prita is a strange name—there can't be too many of them."

"I still don't see why we can't read the letters," Simon complained. "What's the big deal?"

"They're *private*," Delilah insisted. "What if he was her true love?"

"Uncle Hank had tons of girlfriends. What makes you think she's so special?"

"I can just tell." Delilah's chin pushed forward stubbornly. "I think she was . . . the one."

"One what?" Jack demanded.

Henry gathered the other postcards together and looped the string around them, pondering Delilah's comment. "She means the *one*. The one special person he was meant to be with from the very beginning."

"That's ridiculous," Simon scoffed. "The world is full of billions of people. You think there's just ONE right person for each of us?"

"Yes," Delilah answered promptly. "That's what my dad always said."

Henry turned to her in surprise, but she was already picking up the phone, punching a quick series of keys. "Mom? Hey, it's me. I'm at the Barkers'. No, nothing's wrong. Mrs. Barker wants to know if we can come over for dinner tonight. With their aunt Kathy and Emmett

Trask—remember Emmett? Great! Okay, I'll tell her. Yeah, I will. Bye."

She turned back to the boys. "I'll hold on to these," she said, still clamping the packet of letters against her side. "I'm supposed to ask your mom what time we should come and what we should bring." With that, she bounded up the basement stairs.

That night, Aunt Kathy and Emmett showed up with a big yellow bowl of potato salad, and Delilah and her mother brought coleslaw. Mrs. Barker made hamburger patties at the kitchen counter, patting them swiftly into shape and then dropping them on a platter, while Mr. Barker laid out a spread of "fixin's," as he called them—squeeze bottles of ketchup, mustard, and mayonnaise, and a platter of sliced tomatoes, onions, and lettuce leaves.

As soon as Emmett walked out onto the deck, away from the other adults, the boys and Delilah swarmed around him.

"Do you know anybody around here named Prita?" Delilah asked.

"Sure," Emmett said. "Prita Alchesay."

Delilah elbowed Henry smugly. "Those were the

initials!" she whispered. "PA." Henry grinned back at her. How could it be so easy? They would find her after all.

"You know her?" Simon asked in disbelief.

"I sure do."

"That's a funny name," Jack said.

"Not really," Emmett replied. "It's Apache."

Jack bounced on his toes. "Apache! INDIAN? Is she a real live Indian?"

Emmett laughed. "Yes, Jack. There are lots of real live Indians around here. They lived here before anybody else did, and there are still plenty of people with Apache heritage in this area."

"Cool!" Jack shouted.

"Does she live here in Superstition?" Henry asked.

"Yep. Not far from me, actually." Emmett leaned against the deck railing. "Why?"

"Oh," Simon said nonchalantly, "Uncle Hank was friends with her."

"Huh. Now that you mention it, I remember seeing them together. And it makes sense they would have gotten along."

Before they could pepper him with more questions, Aunt Kathy came tapping over in lime green sandals with very high heels. She was wearing a flowery white and green sundress and carried a tiny purse, in matching green, slung over one arm. She slipped her other arm around Emmett and beamed at him. "Now, what are you all chitchatting about?"

Henry looked at her pink-cheeked, glowing face and realized he had never seen her so happy. These days, whenever she was with Emmett, she looked positively giddy . . . like she was at a carnival and had just stepped off the most fun ride in the world.

"Do you believe that there's one person for everybody?" he asked her suddenly. "A person you're meant to be with?"

Aunt Kathy tilted her head to one side, her eyes sparkling. "Oh, that is such an interesting question. And believe me, I have had this conversation more than once. Are we fated to be with one person? Does everybody have a soul mate? And how about this: will we even recognize that person when we finally meet him?"

Emmett shot her a look of tolerant amusement. "And what do you think?"

"Well, this will probably surprise you, sweetie, but I am a pragmatist at heart," she said, leaning against the railing next to Emmett and resting her head on his shoulder. "I think the belief in 'the one' has caused a lot of people a whole lot of heartache. They wait around expecting to be struck by lightning—love at first sight. They believe they will just KNOW which person is the right one for them. But really, love is not like that. It's a matter of choosing . . . choosing to make someone your one."

Emmett nodded thoughtfully and said to the boys, "Listen to your aunt. She's a genius about this stuff."

"Kathy's a genius?" Mr. Barker interjected, on his way to the grill. "Then I have to hear this."

It occurred to Henry that his father was likely to have an interesting opinion on the matter as well. "Do you believe that there's one person for everybody, Dad?" he asked.

"One person who is your destiny," Delilah clarified.

Simon snorted. "One person out of the seven billion people on the planet."

"Yes," he answered promptly. "But it doesn't always work out, so you have to be willing to settle for second best. Like I did with your mother."

"WHAT???" The boys cried in unison.

"Laura Milner," their father said dreamily.

Mrs. Barker opened the sliding glass door, balancing the platter of hamburger patties on her hip, then following Delilah's mother onto the deck. "Oh heavens, don't get him started on Laura Milner," she said.

"She had the face of an angel." Their father sighed.

Mrs. Barker rolled her eyes. "And the legs of a dancer, don't forget."

Aunt Kathy's laugh rolled through the air in throaty, infectious waves. "Laura Milner! I haven't thought about her in ages."

Henry looked from his father to his mother in total bewilderment. He knew his father had had several girlfriends before he got married—which, frankly, was unsettling enough—but this was the first he'd heard of anybody named Laura Milner.

"You've never talked about her," he said to his father in surprise.

"That's because he never went out with her," Mrs. Barker explained. "She wanted nothing to do with him."

"Well, no matter." Mr. Barker shrugged. "She was the one."

"The one that got away?" Mrs. Dunworthy asked, smiling.

Delilah looked horrified. "If she was the one, how could you let her get away?"

Henry turned to her in reproach. Didn't she realize that if Laura Milner hadn't gotten away, his father would never have married his mother . . . and he, Simon, and Jack would not even exist?

Mrs. Barker laughed. "Oh, Laura Milner got away all right. As fast as she could!"

"And then you were stuck with him," Aunt Kathy said to her sister.

Mrs. Barker smiled. "It was a tough job, but somebody had to do it."

Mr. Barker winked at Henry. "See that? For your mother, I was the one."

Henry decided they were all joking around, as adults were wont to do . . . not taking the question seriously. Simon must have concluded the same thing, because he beckoned to the other kids. "Let's get out of here."

Mr. Barker grabbed his shoulder. "Not so fast, sport. I'm putting the burgers on."

"We'll be right back," Simon promised. He led the way into the kitchen, now vacated by the adults. "We need the phone book," he said in a low voice, as he stood on tiptoe to reach the cabinet above the kitchen phone. "So we can look up her address."

Delilah grabbed Henry's hand and squeezed it. "We're going to meet Uncle Hank's one true love," she whispered. Henry looked at her shyly, feeling a strange warmth flood his cheeks.

"No such thing," Simon snapped. "But"—he opened the slender Superstition phone book and ran his finger down one thin gray page, until he stabbed it triumphantly—"tomorrow we'll go see Prita Alchesay, at forty-nine Ken-tee Court."

CHAPTER 12
PRITA

THE NEXT MORNING, with the sun already a hot white orb in the sky, the boys rode their bikes over to Delilah's. Henry knew it would be another scorching day. Behind the slanted roofs of the houses, he could see the dark, jagged slopes of Superstition Mountain. It was hard to believe they had managed to climb up and down the mountain three times that summer. It was hard to believe they'd managed to climb the mountain and come back at all. So many people never did.

"She lives on Ken-tee Court?" he called to Simon.

Simon nodded. "We'll go down Peralta and then turn left after Delilah's street. It's the dead-end road there."

"The name of her street . . ." Henry began.

"Yeah, I know," Simon said. "I recognize it. It was

someone we read about, wasn't it? The Indian girl who led somebody to the gold mine?"

"That's it," Henry said. "But I can't remember if she was real or a legend."

"She was the one who got her tongue cut out!" Jack yelled. "For telling where the gold was."

Trust Jack to remember that, Henry thought.

Delilah was waiting for them at the end of her driveway, sitting on her bike. "I have the letters," she said, gesturing to the ribbon-tied packet in her wicker bicycle basket.

"I still think we should read them," Simon grumbled. "But maybe this Prita woman will tell us what they say."

"Do you think we should call her house before we go over there?" Henry asked. "If she's as old as Uncle Hank and we just show up, it might scare her."

Jack was already halfway down the block and showed no signs of slowing down.

"I think it's okay," Simon said. "We're just kids. It's not like we're going to rob her. We can always send Delilah to the door."

"Sure, I'll go first," Delilah said agreeably. Henry sensed that she was trying to ingratiate herself with Simon, probably because of their disagreement over the love letters. For some reason, it annoyed him.

A few minutes later, they had reached the end of Ken-tee Court, where a small, peach-colored stucco house stood, surrounded by desert. The house looked neat and quiet. The garage door was closed.

"This is it," Simon said. "Number forty-nine. It doesn't look like anyone's home."

Jack dropped his bike with a clatter next to the mailbox and started up the driveway, but Henry stopped him. "Wait, Jack. Delilah's going first, remember?"

"But I want to see an Indian!" Jack protested.

"You will," Simon assured him, "but only if she lets us in the house. Stay here while Delilah goes to the door."

Delilah snapped down her kickstand with one foot and propped her bike by the edge of the driveway, taking the packet of letters from the basket. The boys watched as she approached the front door. Henry saw her toss her braid back and square her shoulders. She pressed the doorbell.

There was no answer.

Glancing back at them with raised eyebrows, Delilah pressed the doorbell again.

"Maybe she's not here," Henry said.

"Try knocking," Simon suggested.

Delilah made a fist and rapped her knuckles on the door twice, waiting.

After a minute, the door opened partway, and a woman with long silvery hair stood on the threshold. Her face was round and a pretty light brown color, crisscrossed with wrinkles. Her eyes were bright and dark.

"Yes?" she said. "May I help you?"

Henry could see Delilah shift nervously. "Is your name Prita?" she asked. "Prita Alchesay?" She held out the ribbon-tied bundle of blue note cards.

The woman gasped and immediately reached for them. "My letters!" she cried. "Where did you get these?"

"Come on," Simon whispered to Henry and Jack, and they all three walked up the driveway.

"We're Hank Cormody's nephews," Simon called.

"Great-nephews," Henry said.

"Are you a real Indian?" Jack demanded. He looked skeptical.

"Jack!" Simon scolded.

Prita's smile was a wide flash of white across her face, as she held the packet of note cards with both hands against her chest.

"I'm Apache," she told Jack. "Ndee, we call ourselves."

"But you look just like a regular person," Jack complained, and Henry cringed to think that he must have been expecting feathers and tomahawks.

"Well, I am that too," Prita said. "So, you're Hank's family! Come in, come in."

She swung the door open and beckoned them inside her small, tidy house. Henry could feel the cool blast of the air conditioner coming from a room in the back, and she led them toward it, into a glassed-in sunporch that faced Superstition Mountain.

"He spoke of you so often," she said. "Which one of you is Henry?"

Henry's heart leapt. Uncle Hank had told her about him! About *him.*

"I am," he said, looking up at her.

"Oh, I am so glad you came." Her hand rested on his shoulder. "I have something for you, Henry. Your great-uncle asked me to give it to you."

Henry's eyes widened. "What is it?"

"I'll have to find it for you. I know I should have come over to see you long ago, but I . . ." She stopped, then said simply, "It was hard for me to think of going to his house without him there."

Delilah was watching her, a serious look on her face. "You miss him."

"Oh yes. Every single day."

"But how come we've never heard of you?" Jack wanted to know.

It was strange, Henry thought, that Uncle Hank had never mentioned someone who seemed to be such an important part of his life. What did it mean?

Prita sat in a chair near the windows and motioned them toward the two sofas. "Your uncle and I are . . . we were both very . . ." She hesitated. "Private."

Delilah shot Henry a quick, confirming glance.

"We didn't read your letters," Simon said quickly, and Henry thought it was quite clever of him to take credit for that discretion now, when he had been the one who was so determined to read them.

"Thank you. I appreciate that."

"Except for one," Simon said. "There was one that wasn't tied up with the others, and a key fell out of it."

Prita was still holding the little bundle of note cards in her lap. She smoothed the silken ribbon and studied Simon appraisingly, waiting for him to go on.

"We know where the key came from," Simon said.

"It's the key to room six at the Black Cat Hotel in Gold Creek. And you gave it to Uncle Hank."

Prita's eyebrows lifted. She continued to gaze at him silently. Henry noticed that this not-responding was a good way for her to respond, because as the silence yawned into awkwardness, Simon felt compelled to keep talking.

"Julia Thomas's room. Why did you have it?"

"It was given to me a long time ago," Prita said quietly. "By someone who wanted help finding the gold."

"Who?" Henry asked, his voice as quiet as hers. "Who gave it to you?"

"The person is no longer alive."

Henry and Simon exchanged glances.

"What happened—" Henry started to ask, but Simon interrupted him.

"We know you gave Uncle Hank the directions to the Lost Dutchman's Mine—we found the note with your handwriting on it. And we know Uncle Hank went to the gold mine. We just don't know if he ever found the gold."

When Prita said nothing, Simon squirmed. "So . . . do you know if he ever took gold from the mine?"

Prita looked at him steadily. "No, he didn't," she said finally.

Henry leaned forward, scrutinizing her calm face. "But why not?" he asked.

"I convinced him not to."

All four children stared at her.

"Why'd you do that?" Jack demanded. "He would have been RICH!"

Prita shook her head. "No. He would have been dead."

"What do you mean?" Delilah asked. "He *is* dead."

Prita sighed, and gathered her long hair in one hand, twisting it over her shoulder. She stared out the window, her eyes tracing the dark silhouette of Superstition

Mountain. "He would have died sooner. A bad death. A death full of suffering."

Henry felt a chill of foreboding, and he knew what she was going to say before she said it. She turned back to them. "You don't know the mountain. The mountain is sacred. Anyone who takes gold from that mine will die."

CHAPTER 13
THE DEADLY CURSE

ALL HENRY COULD THINK of was the handful of tiny gold flakes that Jack had taken from the gold mine. Jack's eyes were enormous. His lower lip quivered. "Even a little gold?" he asked.

"Any gold from the mine," Prita answered. "To the Thunder God, the amount does not matter."

"But . . ." Jack's cheeks were splotched with color. Henry could tell he was on the verge of tears.

Delilah glanced over at him and said quickly, "What if it's not nuggets of gold, just little bits? Just . . . gold dust?"

Prita shook her head. "It doesn't matter. Anyone who takes gold from the mine will die."

Jack could no longer contain himself. "I'm going to

DIE!" he cried. He flung himself on the floor, his arms covering his face, his body wracked with sobs.

Henry quickly crouched beside him, not knowing what to do. But Simon was there too, pulling him up.

"Come on, Jack," Simon said, and his voice was calm, not scolding. "You know that's not real. Curses and ghosts, they're just made-up things. You're not going to die. That's crazy."

"I'm going to DIE!" Jack sobbed. "You heard what she said!"

Prita knelt on the floor and gathered Jack, big as he was, into her lap. "What happened? What did you do?" she asked gently.

"I took gold from the mine! I didn't know!" Jack cried, turning his face into her shoulder and sobbing unabashedly. "Now I'm going to be DEAD!"

Henry could see a dark, wet stain spreading across Prita's blouse.

She held Jack close. "Then you must return it," she said simply. "That's what I told your uncle to do.".

Jack stopped crying, though he still hiccupped. "You said Uncle Hank didn't take gold." He gulped.

"Well, he didn't keep it. He put it back."

"Uncle Hank took the gold too?"

Prita nodded, setting him gently on the floor. "Let me get you a glass of water," she said.

A minute later, she returned with a blue plastic cup and a box of tissues. Jack took the cup gratefully and guzzled it, still snuffling. Delilah wiped off his cheeks with the tissues, and Henry was surprised to see him submit to it so docilely.

Prita sat back down in the chair and said, "That's how your uncle and I first met."

"When was that?" Simon asked.

Prita's brow furrowed and she glanced out the window. "It was twelve years ago."

Before any of us were born, Henry thought.

"He was looking for the gold mine," Prita continued, "and he knew I was descended from Ken-tee, the Ndee—Apache—girl who first showed Jacob Waltz where the gold was. I warned him about the Thunder God, but he didn't believe me."

"You're related to Ken-tee?" Henry asked. "The girl whose tongue was cut out? Your street is named for her."

"Yes," Prita said. "She is one of my ancestors."

"So what happened?" Simon asked. "You gave Uncle Hank the directions to the gold mine?"

"Yes. In the note you found."

"But why did you do that?" Henry asked. "You said if he took gold from the mine, the Thunder God would kill him."

Prita sighed, and looked out the window again. "There is too much for me to explain. I helped him because he said he wanted to find the mine, not take the gold. Your uncle was an adventurer. He didn't care about material things. He told me he didn't want the gold . . . but then, as it does for everyone, the search for the gold began to change him."

"Was it gold fever?" Henry asked. He remembered Emmett telling them about gold fever, the mania that infected people who searched for the gold mine until the gold became more important to them than anyone or anything else.

"Yes," Prita answered. "It's an obsession. The desire for the gold makes people crazy—it becomes the only thing they can think about."

"So when he found the mine, he did take gold from it?" Simon asked.

"Yes, he took a few small nuggets, even though he had promised me he wouldn't. By then, we had become . . . close." She was talking to herself now. "The gold, the

gold . . . it was the only thing we ever fought about. I told him I would not see him anymore if he kept it."

"So he took it back," Delilah said, satisfied. "Because he loved you."

"But does that work?" Henry asked. "If you take back the gold, the curse is undone?"

"Yes," Prita said. "Returning the gold to the mine appeases the Thunder God. So, for me, Hank went back up the mountain and returned it. And that's when he began searching for the deathbed ore of Jacob Waltz instead."

Simon shook his head, puzzled. "The deathbed ore? But that's still gold from the mine, right? Why does that make a difference? It's stolen from the mountain too."

"Yes," Prita answered. "But the Thunder God only punishes the one who takes. When that person is gone and the mountain's gold passes into other hands, the curse doesn't follow it."

Jack's lower lip quivered. "When that person is GONE," he whispered.

"So your uncle Hank began his search for the candle box of gold nuggets that Jacob Waltz kept under his bed and that disappeared when he died."

Henry was lost in thought, his mind wandering over the long list of names in the pamphlet from the historical society. "That's why all those people died? Jacob Waltz, Adolph Ruth, and the others?"

Prita shook her head. "The mountain is a dangerous place. Many people have died there, and not all of them found the gold. But for those who did . . . yes. That is the curse of the Thunder God. Anyone who takes the mountain's gold must die."

Jack was still snuffling, watching her with large, wet eyes. "But I can just give it back? How do you know that will work?"

Prita pulled him toward her so she could look directly at him. "It is what my great-grandmother told me, and what was told to her by Ken-tee," she said intently. "I wasn't sure it would work until Hank did it. But he took the nuggets back to the mine, and he lived his long life. There was no suffering, no early death."

"And he couldn't have just given the gold to you?" Simon asked skeptically. "Giving it away isn't enough?"

"No. The Thunder God's curse follows the one who stole the gold," she said simply. "And as I told him, if the gold were to be stolen from him, he would have no way to reverse the curse."

"Was somebody trying to steal the gold from him?" Simon looked suddenly alert.

"He believed so, yes," Prita said. "He thought he was being followed."

"Who was it?" Simon asked, but Henry was certain they already knew the answer.

"There are people in this town who are desperate to find the mine and the gold," Prita said.

"Who?" Simon persisted.

"I doubt you would know them," Prita said. "One works at the library. One works at the cemetery."

Simon nodded grimly. "We know them."

"'Cuz they're following us too!" Jack turned to Simon, his face desperate. "We have to go back up the mountain! Back to the gold mine! Before they take my gold and the curse STICKS."

"Well, I still don't think that curse is real," Simon said stubbornly, and then, as Jack's eyes filled with tears, he continued quickly, "But okay, okay. We'll take it back. If even the littlest thing does happen to you, I don't want you blaming it on me. So I guess we don't have a choice."

Jack's face shone with relief. "But then we'll never be rich," he said, sorrowfully.

Henry could picture the dark, damp walls of the mine, streaked with sparkling gold. Did that mean the gold was lost to them forever?

Simon didn't look happy. "But there's no curse on the deathbed ore? That box of gold from Jacob Waltz?"

Prita shook her head. "No. After Jacob Waltz died, it was freed from the curse. That's why Hank began looking for that instead."

"And he never found it?" Delilah asked.

Prita smiled. "It really was the looking that mattered to him, more than the finding. But that reminds me! Henry, let me get you what your uncle left for you."

She rested her palms on the arm of the chair and rose to her feet. "I'll be right back."

As soon as she was gone, Delilah said to Simon, "See? I was right about those letters. Prita and your uncle Hank were in love."

Simon snorted. "Maybe. But who cares? We have bigger things to worry about than that. What good is it finding the Lost Dutchman's Mine if we can't take any of the gold?"

Prita returned with a sealed envelope in her hand. Henry immediately recognized Uncle Hank's creamy stationery. The envelope was emblazoned with his name in black script: *Henry Cormody*. It matched the stationery they had found in his desk drawer when they first moved to his house in Superstition; the same stationery

Henry Cormody

Josie had found crumpled in the gold mine, which had convinced them that Uncle Hank had been there and found the gold.

"Here, Henry," Prita said, holding it out to him.

Henry took it, his fingers trembling. Uncle Hank had left him a message, something only and especially for him—something Uncle Hank had written before he died. What could it possibly say?

Jack bounced forward onto his knees. "Did he leave anything for me? Or Simon?" he asked Prita.

"No, just this. For Henry," Prita said.

And even as Henry's heart leapt at the feeling of being

chosen, he felt a pang of guilt over his brothers, who were sitting next to him empty-handed.

He held the cool envelope in his palm.

"Open it," Simon ordered.

"Yeah, open it!" Jack echoed.

Henry looked at Prita. She nodded silently.

He tore open the sealed flap of the envelope and slowly took out what was inside.

CHAPTER 14
SOMETHING FOR HENRY

INSIDE THE CREAMY ENVELOPE was a folded sheet of paper. When Henry opened it, he saw HENRY CORMODY in the same black script across the top, and felt again the thrill of seeing his own first name in such a dignified and formal fashion. Beneath that were a few bold lines of Uncle Hank's handwriting, instantly recognizable from years of birthday cards. *He wrote this before he died*, Henry thought. *He wrote this for me.*

"Read it to us!" Jack cried, bouncing excitedly. "What does it say?"

Henry squinted at the page. Even though the ink writing was large and dark, it was cursive, and the lines were a little shaky.

"*Dear Henry*," he read aloud, and felt a chill pierce

him. It was like hearing Uncle Hank's voice from beyond the grave.

"*Dear Henry,*" he read again, concentrating on the spare lines of text. "*Your name is my name. It will outlast death—the way a place can be about death but outlast death. If you believe that, you'll know where to find something I left for you and your brothers. Live well, Henry. Love, Uncle Hank.*"

"See? You and YOUR BROTHERS," Jack declared. "It's for us too." He jabbed Simon with his elbow.

"Huh," Simon said. "I wonder what it is. Did he say anything to you?"

"No," Prita said. "He only left me the envelope, to give to Henry. I'm sorry I didn't do it sooner. You moved in a few weeks ago, didn't you?"

"It's been more than two months," Henry said. "The beginning of June."

"I didn't realize it had been that long." Her face clouded. "I'm sorry."

"It doesn't matter," Henry told her quickly. "I'm just glad we found you." Looking into her calm, dark eyes, he did feel truly glad. This was someone Uncle Hank had loved. Whether she was what Simon thought—just one girlfriend of many—or what Delilah thought—the love

of his life—she was someone who had been important to him. That alone made Henry feel a connection to her.

"What do you think it means?" Delilah asked. She took the letter from Henry's hand and read it to herself. *"It will outlast death. . . ."*

"Well, that's obvious," Simon said. "Of course his name will outlast death, because Henry is named for him. But if he left something for us, that doesn't tell us where it would be."

Delilah handed the letter back to Henry. "Did he leave you guys anything in his will?"

Henry shook his head. "The house was for our whole family."

"A house is a place that outlasts someone's death," Prita said. "Was there anything at Hank's house that had your name on it? When you moved in, I mean?"

Again, Henry shook his head. "We've been through the drawers of his desk—that's where we found your letters. And our mom and dad boxed up all his belongings. They would have told us if they found anything he meant for us to have."

Delilah tossed her braid over one shoulder and squinted through the bright windows of the sunporch at Superstition Mountain, looming in the distance. "We need to think of someplace that is *about* death but *out-lasts* death," she said. "A mountain outlasts death. Think of all the people who have died on Superstition Mountain, either looking for the gold or just getting lost or killed up there. But the mountain is still there."

Simon's brows knitted together skeptically. "If Uncle Hank left something for us on the mountain, we will never find it. The mountain is too big! We wouldn't know where to look."

"Well," Henry said, "he did leave the directions to the gold mine. And the Spanish coins that we found."

Prita took Jack's empty water cup. "I can promise you he would not have meant for you to take anything from the gold mine," she said. "He knew how dangerous that was. He returned the gold he took, and he would never have wanted any of you boys to put your lives at risk."

She returned the cup to the kitchen and came back, studying them. "He loved you," she said finally.

They were quiet. Henry was thinking about Uncle Hank, with his wild, adventurous heart that had loved this woman they'd never met, along with his great-nephews.

"Okay," Delilah said. "Then not the mountain."

Henry rubbed his forehead, his cheeks hot with

concentration. What could Uncle Hank have meant?
Lots of Uncle Hank's belongings had outlasted his death,
so that wasn't saying anything. But you couldn't *expect*
objects to outlast a person's life. Most things didn't last
as long as people. There were Uncle Hank's ashes—
they'd lasted longer than Uncle Hank, Henry thought
soberly—but since Uncle Hank had obviously been cremated *after* he died, it would have been impossible for
him to leave anything for the boys in the porcelain urn
full of ashes.

"Wait," Henry said suddenly. "A place that is *about death* but *outlasts death* . . . I think I know what it is!"

They all turned to him. "What?" Simon asked.

Henry could feel his face burning with excitement. "The cemetery!"

CHAPTER 15
GRAVE DEVELOPMENTS

DELILAH'S EYES WIDENED with recognition. "The cemetery!"

But Simon frowned. "I don't see how that can be it. There's no grave for Uncle Hank at the cemetery."

"No," Prita said. "He did consider being buried there, but then he decided he wanted to be cremated."

"He talked to you about that?" Henry asked, surprised.

"Oh yes," she answered with a small smile. "We talked about everything. He called me his dear one." At their puzzled expressions, she added, "It's what my name means, in Apache. *Prita* is 'dear one.'"

"It's a nice name," Delilah said.

Simon got to his feet. "But he *was* cremated. So there shouldn't be anything at the cemetery."

"I know," Henry said. "I thought about that. It's just . . . a cemetery is the . . . *ultimate* place that outlasts death, because it's all about death, but the graves and the tombstones are what survive after someone is gone. You know?"

He knew he wasn't explaining it well. But he remembered bicycling past the cemetery on the way to the ghost town, past the bright, orderly rows of crosses and monuments, and the impression he had of it being a place teeming with life—with the past lives of all the people who were now buried there.

"We should go back and have another look around," Delilah said. "Maybe we'll find something he left there for us—for you," she corrected, looking at Henry.

"And me too!" Jack interjected. "And Simon. Just not you."

Simon ran his hand through his hair, roughing it into spiky clumps. "Unless . . ."

"Unless what?" Henry asked.

"Well, Prita says he was thinking of being buried at the cemetery. What if he owned a plot there?"

"What does that mean?" Jack demanded. "What's a plot?"

"For people to be buried in a cemetery, they have to

purchase a piece of the land," Prita told him. "And then that's where their grave will be. I don't see why Hank would have done that if he intended to be cremated. But your uncle was full of surprises."

"It's worth checking," Simon decided. "We should head home now." He wiped his hands on his shorts and held one out to Prita. "It was nice to meet you," he said, and Henry thought he sounded suddenly shy.

She ignored his hand and drew him into a hug, her long silver hair falling over him. "I am so happy to meet all of you," she answered, her voice warm. "I know we will see each other again."

She stroked Jack's hair and said, "Return the gold, and everything will be fine."

When it was Henry's turn, she cupped her slim brown hands on either side of his face and looked steadily into his eyes. "Henry," she said. "The namesake! Live well."

It was exactly what Uncle Hank had said in his letter, which made it the second time Henry had been told that in one day, and he wasn't even sure what it meant.

"We'll come visit you again," Delilah promised, as they left Prita's front stoop and started to head down the driveway.

"And you'll have to come to our house," Henry said.

"Uncle Hank's house." He added, "When it doesn't make you sad anymore."

"I would like that," Prita said. She lifted her hand to wave as they hopped onto their bikes and rode away, down Ken-tee Court.

That afternoon, they gathered in the kitchen to discuss their return to the cemetery. Conveniently, their mother had gone to the grocery store; they had the house to themselves and could talk freely. Henry had tucked Uncle Hank's note safely in the drawer of his nightstand and was now pouring frosty glasses of lemonade for everyone, while Simon slapped together ham and cheese sandwiches. Delilah held Josie on her lap, stroking her flat, triangular head. Josie purred contentedly.

"I wonder where we can find information about who owns the grave plots," Simon said, spreading mustard on four slices of bread. "It would be better not to have to ask that caretaker Mr. Delgado. You know he'll report back to the librarian and Officer Myers about what we're doing."

"Do you think there are records anywhere else, besides at the cemetery?" Delilah asked.

"I don't know. I doubt it." Simon assembled the

sandwiches and sliced them diagonally, piling them on a plate in the middle of the table. Henry carried the glasses over from the counter, and they all clustered around to eat.

After a bit, Henry said, "It seems like there might be a record for the historic graves."

"That's true," Simon allowed, "but how does that help us? We're interested in a grave plot that Uncle Hank would have purchased in the last ten years or so. Right?"

"Yeah," Henry said, wiping the crumbs from his mouth. "But maybe we should ask Emmett. He had to find the location of Julia Thomas's grave in Phoenix, remember? I bet he'll know what to do."

"Good idea. Let's call him," Simon said. He wiped his hands on his shorts and grabbed the phone book from the cupboard, sliding it across the table to Henry.

Jack thumped his hand on top of it, holding it firm. "No, wait," he protested. "When are we going back up the mountain? To return the gold. We have to do that first! Before I DIE."

"You know we can't do that while Mom and Dad are around," Simon said.

"When, then?" Jack demanded, holding tight to the

phone book. "That's more important than going back to that old graveyard."

Simon turned to Henry. "Didn't they say they're doing something with Emmett and Aunt Kathy on Sunday?"

Henry did vaguely remember that. "Yeah, I think so. They're going into Phoenix to the art museum, right? But I thought they wanted us to go with them."

"We can probably get out of it," Simon said. "We'll stay and clean out the garage. Mom's been wanting us to do that."

The garage! Henry shuddered. It was full of moving boxes that were packed with their outdoor toys and games from Illinois—volleyball, croquet, sidewalk chalk—not to mention the various tools and yard implements that Mr. Barker hadn't needed yet . . . saws, wrenches, hedge trimmers. "That'll take a really long time," Henry said dubiously.

"I'll help you," Delilah offered. "I'm good at organizing stuff."

"Then we can clean the garage in the morning, and go up the mountain in the afternoon," Simon announced.

Jack shook his head vigorously. "That's two whole days away!"

"Jack, listen," Simon said firmly. "The curse probably isn't even real. You've had that gold for weeks now, and you've been fine."

Jack's face began to crumple. "You don't care whether or not I DIE!" he wailed.

"Of course I do," Simon said calmly. "And we'll take the gold back, I promise. But we're going to the cemetery first."

"That's easy for you to say," Jack grumbled. "You're not the one who's cursed."

Henry tried to calm him down. "It's okay, Jack. We can't go until Sunday anyway. And don't you want to try to find whatever it is Uncle Hank left for us?"

"Yeah," Jack said. "Before I DIE."

"You're not going to die," Henry said. "We won't let you."

As soon as he said it, Delilah glanced at him strangely. He thought of her father, killed in a car accident. Instantly, he regretted what he'd said, which sounded like you could protect someone from dying through sheer effort or will.

He looked at her apologetically and pried the phone book loose from Jack's fingers. "Let me call Emmett and see what he says."

Henry dialed the number, and the phone rang and rang. He was almost ready to hang up when a breathless Aunt Kathy answered.

"Oh, hi, hon," she said. "We're just walking in the door from the library. What's going on?"

"Can I talk to Emmett for a minute? We need to ask him something."

"Sure. Something about rocks? My smart boyfriend! He is a veritable encyclopedia."

"No, not rocks," Henry said. "Something about graves."

"*Graves?* You know, I am beginning to think you boys are a little obsessed with death." She laughed her ringing laugh. "Your interests are so *macabre*. . . . That's a good word for you, Henry. It means gruesome. Here's Emmett."

Macabre, Henry repeated to himself. It was a good word for their entire summer, he decided—the steady parade of skulls and bones and curses and graves. When Emmett answered, Henry said without preamble, "Hey, Emmett, we think Uncle Hank might own a plot in the cemetery and we wondered how we could find out. Can you tell us how you found Julia Thomas's grave in Phoenix?"

"Sure, but I thought you said your uncle was cremated," Emmett said.

"He was. We think he might have gotten a cemetery plot for a different reason."

"Really?" Emmett sounded perplexed, and Henry was grateful he didn't ask more questions. "Well, you'll have to go down to the cemetery and look at the records. They're in the office at the caretaker's cottage. Richard Delgado can help you."

Henry hesitated. "We were sort of hoping to avoid him . . . because of the historical society and the treasure hunting and all."

"Does he even know who you are?"

Henry squirmed, gripping the phone. "Yeah. He knows."

"Oh," Emmett said. "Well, he's not there right now anyway. Kathy and I just saw him over at the library, talking to Julia Thomas. Who knows what they're up to. But his daughter, Sara, should be there, and she can show you where to look."

"Sara?" Henry asked doubtfully. "She always seems so out of it." He remembered Sara babbling nonsensically to them that day at the cemetery, and Emmett saying that although she'd always been a strange girl, shy and difficult to talk to, after she was lost for days on Superstition Mountain she had seemed even stranger, as if the mountain had confused the wiring in her brain. She'd come back from the mountain in a fugue state, with no memory of what had happened to her there.

"I don't think she's out of it, exactly," Emmett said. "She can be very observant. She just doesn't communicate the way the rest of us do."

"But you think she could show us how to figure out if Uncle Hank owned a cemetery plot?"

"Sure. The records are in a vertical file cabinet in the front of the office. The list is indexed two ways, by plot location and by last name, so it shouldn't be hard."

"Thanks, Emmett," Henry said with relief.

He hung up the phone and relayed the information quickly to the others. "And if we go now, Mr. Delgado won't be there. Emmett and Aunt Kathy just saw him at the library. So Sara can help us instead."

"That crazy girl?" Jack asked. "We couldn't even talk to her last time."

"Maybe we won't have to," Delilah said, "if the office is open and she'll let us look at the files."

Henry agreed that it might be difficult to communicate

with Sara. But it was still far better than having to deal with her suspicious father.

"Good, let's go before Mr. Delgado gets back," Simon said.

They quickly gulped down the rest of their lemonade and raced out the door.

CHAPTER 16
UNDERSTANDING SARA

THEY RODE PAST THE MAIN ENTRANCE to the cemetery and steered into the small paved parking lot by the caretaker's cottage. There were no cars outside, and the house looked quiet and empty.

"What if Sara's not here either?" Delilah asked.

But before Henry could answer her, the front door swung open and Sara appeared, her long brown hair hanging on either side of her pale face, nearly hiding it. Her eyes darted over them furtively, then looked away.

"You've been here before," she said.

"Hi, Sara," Simon said, and Henry could tell he was trying to sound normal. "Yeah, we met you a few weeks ago. We wondered if you could help us look something up. We think our uncle may have purchased a grave plot here."

"He is in a better place," Sara murmured.

"Oh, brother," Jack whispered to Henry. "Here we go again."

"Do you have somewhere you keep the records of who owns which plot?" Henry asked her.

Sara looked at him and nodded, motioning them inside.

"Everything is as it should be," she said, as she led them into a small office area.

"Here? In the file cabinet?" Simon asked, tapping on the front of a metal drawer.

Sara nodded, taking a piece of paper from a stack on the desk and handing it to Henry. "It is not for us to know. We are not given answers, only questions."

Henry saw that the paper was a photocopied map of the cemetery, with each plot clearly delineated and numbered.

"Well, we were kind of hoping for answers," Simon told her, but Henry noticed that his voice was gentle. He seemed to be trying not to scare her. "Can we look through the files?"

Sara opened the drawer to the file cabinet and turned to him expectantly.

"Alphabetical!" Simon exclaimed. "Great. This shouldn't be too hard."

"Great!" Sara echoed, clapping her hands.

Delilah was watching Sara, her expression thoughtful. "Is your father coming home soon?" she asked.

"Yes, yes," Sara murmured, distractedly tugging at strands of her long hair. "He will come with the others."

Simon looked at her sharply. "The others? Who's with him?"

"The policeman and the librarian," Sara said. "No one is ever really gone."

Yikes! Henry thought. They didn't have much time.

He studied the cemetery map. By orienting it correctly, he could see where the old section of graves was, where they had found the tombstone of Julia Elena Thomas. "We can also look things up by plot," he told Simon, holding the map aloft. "We should see who purchased that Julia Thomas grave, and when."

"Good idea." Simon was thumbing quickly through the manila folders that bulged from the file drawer. "Here are the *C*'s. Hang on. . . ."

Henry felt a tingling beneath his skin, a combination of excitement and foreboding. What if it was there? What if Uncle Hank had purchased a cemetery plot even though he planned to be cremated? Did it mean he had left something for the boys here in the cemetery?

On the other hand, what if it *wasn't* there? Henry considered Uncle Hank's message. He could think of nowhere else that so clearly constituted a place that was about death but would outlast death.

"Here it is! Cormody!" Simon cried, and Henry felt a shiver flow through him.

Simon pulled one folder from the tightly packed row and flipped it open, eagerly scanning the contents. "You were right, Hen. Uncle Hank *did* buy a plot. . . . Look— Henry Cormody." Simon tapped his finger on a densely typed form, with Uncle Hank's bold signature coursing across the bottom.

"When did he buy it?" Delilah asked.

Simon's eyes raced over the page. "The purchase date is two years ago."

"Let's go find it!" Jack shouted.

"Do you have the number of the plot?" Henry asked. "I'll look it up on the map."

"It's thirty-one."

Henry flattened the map on the desk, and they all hunched over it, squinting at the tiny rectangles that covered the paper.

"Here it is," Henry said, pointing. The 31 marked a

rectangle in a tight grid of plots in the far corner of the cemetery.

"Things are never what they seem," Sara Delgado murmured, still twisting her hair.

Simon glanced at her. "It's okay, Sara," he said. "You helped us."

"There's nothing anyone can do," Sara whispered, sounding sad.

Henry felt it too, suddenly; the accretion of losses. What had happened to all of these people whose names stuffed the file cabinet? They all had graves here. They all had ended up in this place. Well, all except Uncle Hank.

Simon was frowning at the map. "Huh. That corner is where the old graves are, isn't it?"

"Where the Julia Thomas tombstone was?" Delilah studied the grid. "Can you look that one up?"

"I'll only be able to find it if she purchased it under her own name," Simon said. "If she didn't, we'd have to know the plot number for the tombstone and look it up in reverse."

"Try," Henry urged.

Simon returned to the file cabinet, thumbing through the manila folders. "There are a couple Thomases, but no Julia," he said after a minute. "Wait . . . what was her husband's name again?"

Henry tried to remember. Was she still married when she was taking care of the ailing Jacob Waltz? Henry couldn't recall what Emmett had said.

"Emil," Delilah said. Henry looked at her in astonishment, but she only shrugged. "I remember stuff like that."

"Emil Thomas!" Simon echoed, waving another folder aloft. "Let's see which plot this is." He opened the folder on the desk and smoothed the thin yellow paper, stained and marbled with age, splotched with fountain-pen ink. "Plot twenty-seven," he said. "And it was purchased in 1889, so that would make sense. It's right near Uncle Hank's. Henry, mark them on the map."

Henry took a ballpoint pen from a canister on the desk and carefully drew circles around the two grave plots.

"But why would she have TWO graves?" Jack demanded.

Sara gathered the folders and started to replace them in the file drawer. "Everyone wants to know that."

The boys and Delilah looked at each other in surprise.

"What do you mean?" Delilah asked her.

Sara slammed the top drawer shut with a bang, holding Emil Thomas's folder under one arm. "Two graves, two graves," she murmured, almost as if she were reciting a rhyme. "Why did she have two graves?"

Delilah tried again. "Who wants to know about Julia Thomas's grave?"

Sara laughed a strange, high laugh. "The one who's buried there! She wants to know herself."

"Do you mean Julia Thomas, the librarian?" Henry asked carefully.

Sara smiled at him. "Two graves, two graves. What's in the second grave?"

Delilah took her arm gently. "Sara."

But Sara pulled open the third drawer of the metal file cabinet and bent over it with the folder, wedging it back into the section of *T*'s.

"They'll find out tonight," she said, straightening. She looked directly at Delilah. "The dead will be raised."

Henry felt a chill beneath his skin.

"Look," Sara said, swinging her hair back from her face, her eyes darting to the window. "Here they come now."

CHAPTER 17

TOMBSTONES BY MOONLIGHT

THEY RUSHED OVER TO THE WINDOW, following Sara's gaze through the dusty panes. Henry almost expected to see the long-dead occupants of the cemetery stirring up from their graves. But instead, he noticed in the distance a brown sedan trundling down the road toward the cemetery.

"Who is that?" Simon turned to Sara. "Is it your father coming back?"

"No one is ever really gone," Sara said. She continued to tidy the office, moving absently around the desk.

"Sara," Delilah said, and again, Sara looked directly at her. "Are they coming here tonight? To dig up the grave of Julia Thomas? Is that what you meant?"

"The dead will be raised," Sara repeated.

"We have to get out of here," Henry said. "Before

they see us." He stared into Sara's wild, dark eyes. "Please don't tell anyone we were here. They . . ." He hesitated, not knowing how to explain why. It was her father, after all. Would she keep their visit a secret from him? He took a deep breath. "They wouldn't understand."

"Nobody understands," Sara said. "Nobody ever understands."

"Come on, let's go," Simon urged. "Thanks, Sara. Thanks for helping us find the graves."

Her brown eyes flickered toward him and she nodded.

The boys and Delilah nearly trampled each other in their effort to get out of the office. Henry had the cemetery map in his hand, with faint blue circles around plot numbers thirty-one and twenty-seven. They ran to the parking area, where they'd dumped their bikes, and quickly threw their legs over the seats.

"They'll see us if we ride out the way we came," Delilah said. "And what if Mr. Delgado has Julia Thomas and Officer Myers in the car with him?"

"Go behind the house," Simon said. "Quickly! We'll ride through the field behind the cemetery."

"Not on the pavement?" Jack moaned. "That's how I cut my knee!"

"I know, Jack," Simon answered impatiently. "But we don't have any choice. Would you rather bump into the librarian?"

"No," Jack grumbled, following Simon over the rough terrain.

Henry steered around a cactus and pedaled harder to keep his balance over the uneven desert. They rode along the wrought-iron fence that enclosed the cemetery, with the bright rows of tombstones marching past them. Henry could see the brown car continuing down the road to the house, almost to the driveway now. It was not until they turned behind the cemetery that he breathed a sigh of relief. Here was a border of high flowering bushes that fully concealed them.

Simon slowed down and dropped one leg to the ground, peering through the bushes.

"Do you think they saw us?" Delilah asked him.

"I hope not," Simon said grimly. "And I hope Sara won't tell them we were there."

"I don't think she will," Henry said after a minute. "Or if she does, I don't think they'll take it seriously. She seems so confused."

Delilah was silent. Finally, she said, "She's not confused

about the way people talk after someone dies. She knows exactly what they say."

"Yeah," Jack said. "She's always saying stuff about dead people!"

Henry shuddered. "Maybe the mountain made her like that."

"No, it didn't, Hen," Simon corrected him. "You heard Emmett. He said she was always strange."

"Well, she told us something important about tonight," Delilah interrupted them. "It sounds like the librarian and Officer Myers are coming here to help Mr. Delgado dig up Julia Thomas's grave! What if they find the gold from under Jacob Waltz's bed? The deathbed ore?"

Simon frowned. "Before we do? We can't let them."

"Simon," Henry said, "we can't do anything to stop them. They're at the house right now, or at least Mr. Delgado is. If he catches us messing around in the cemetery, who knows what he'll do to us. And he'll definitely figure out what we're up to."

"Yeah," Simon said in disappointment. "You're right. But we can't let them take the gold! Not after all our hard work. If we can't get the gold from the Lost Dutchman's Mine, at least we have to find the deathbed ore. We're coming to the cemetery tonight."

"Yeah!" Jack yelled. "We can watch them dig up the grave!"

Delilah hung back, her hands gripping the handlebars of her bicycle. "I don't think that's right, digging up graves," she said, lips pursed. "What if the gold's not even there? Somebody might be buried in that grave."

"I guess we'll find out tonight," Henry said soberly. He glanced through the black iron fence at the stark rows of tombstones quietly staring back at them. If the cemetery felt spooky during the day, how was it going to feel at night . . . with a bunch of grave robbers in it?

Lost in their private thoughts, they continued the hot ride home, across the rough desert, with the dark bluffs of Superstition Mountain rising in the distance.

After a hurried dinner, the boys were all back on their bikes, riding to Delilah's and then the cemetery. It was a little after seven o'clock and the sky was streaked with pink as the sun slid to the horizon. The desert looked strange at night, Henry thought; a lunar landscape of boulders and spires, with even the ordinary suburban houses rising from the dust like bastions of some alien civilization. He thought of one of his favorite books, *A Wrinkle in Time*, which took place on another planet.

Josie was in the front yard as the boys left, stalking something in the grass. The commotion of the bikes broke her concentration, and she stared at them in disgust, her amber eyes glowing in the fading light. Henry saw her start to follow them, darting after Jack's bike. But then she disappeared into the bramble of the desert, the white splotch on her neck flashing in the darkness.

"What if Sara Delgado just made all that up, and they're not coming tonight?" Delilah asked. Though the light was dusky, Henry could see the worried expression on her face.

"I brought the map," Henry told her, patting his front pocket. "If they don't show up, we can look for Uncle Hank's grave plot."

"In the dark?" Delilah sounded skeptical.

"Sure!" Simon called. "I have a flashlight."

"We're going to need it," Jack said. "It will be spooky dark there."

"Okay, quiet," Simon said. "That's the cemetery ahead. We can hide our bikes in the bushes on the side."

Henry thought the gravel made an inordinate amount of noise as they pedaled toward the wrought-iron fence. Simon led the way off the road and over the sandy ground, toward the bushes. Quickly, they stashed their bicycles behind the shrubbery, then snuck along the fence to the front gates.

"Uh-oh," Jack whispered. "They're locked."

"Locked?" Simon repeated in surprise.

"Now what do we do?" Delilah asked. "They probably lock the gates at sunset."

Again, Henry noticed how much she seemed to know about this sort of thing, and he felt a stab of sadness for all the things she must have had to learn after her father died.

"Okay, we'll have to try to climb the fence," Simon said. "In the back, where nobody can see us. Follow me."

He raced along the side of the fence, his sneakers crunching over the pebbly desert. The sun had almost vanished now, and the violet dusk was darkening all around them. "We'll go to that area where the old graves are. So we can climb over the fence right where we want to be."

"I don't know," Henry said softly, scanning the wrought-iron posts. "It's pretty high. How are we going to climb it?"

"We'll use the bushes, and my shirt if we have to," Simon said, unperturbed.

When they got to the back corner of the cemetery where the older graves were clustered, Simon boldly clambered over the bushes and reached for a finial in the evenly spaced row that bordered the top of the fence. He was able to grab one and haul himself upward, pressing the soles of his sneakers against the vertical rungs of the fence. When he got to the top, he straddled the thick bar that ran along the top.

"Wow, I can see everything from up here," he told them. "The lights are on in the house, and that brown car is in the driveway . . . next to a police car!"

"Officer Myers," Delilah said.

"Yeah, I bet. But nobody's in the cemetery." Simon adjusted his position. "Oww," he said, under his breath. "Here, Delilah, give me your hand. I'll help you."

Delilah climbed over the bushes and gamely extended her arm. Simon grasped her wrist with one hand and her elbow with the other, then yanked her upward. "Whoa . . ." Delilah cried, as they both toppled over the spiky top of the fence and half climbed, half fell, in a muddle of arms and legs on the other side.

"Oops," Simon said, and they both started laughing. "We're in!"

"Shhhhh!" Henry hushed them. "We have to be quiet." He watched them resentfully. How was he going to get over the fence now that Simon was on the other side? Was he going to have to help Jack? Or worse yet, ask Jack for help, which would be embarrassing in front of Delilah? And why hadn't he gone first and helped Delilah over the fence? He sighed, thinking that Simon always seemed to be in the right place at the right time.

"Okay, now you, Hen."

"No, I want to go next!" Jack cried, barreling over the shrubs and throwing himself against the fence. He couldn't reach the finials, but by grabbing the rungs, he managed to pull himself up to the top, where he threw a leg over.

"Wait, Jack," Henry said desperately. "If you pull me up, I can hold on to you as you go down the other side, so you don't fall."

"Okay," Jack agreed, reaching down for Henry's hand. The branches of the bushes were trampled and broken now from the weight of three trespassers. Henry couldn't get nearly high enough to grab the top of the fence, but with Jack's help, he managed to haul himself up and straddle the top bar. Then he held Jack's hand as Jack descended into the cemetery.

"Can you get down by yourself?" Delilah asked, standing below him.

"Sure," Henry said, brushing her off, though he didn't feel at all sure. He glanced around from his high vantage point, the cold metal bar gripped between his legs. The tombstones unfolded in their silent, orderly rows beneath him. The night was turning blue, and a glowing half moon lit the field of graves. Henry gazed toward the caretaker's cottage. He saw the brown sedan and the police car, its town logo shining officially. As he watched, the door to the house swung open, and a long rectangle of light filled the small yard. A large, shadowy figure blocked the doorway, and Henry could hear the distant murmur of voices.

"Wait," Henry whispered. "They're coming out of the house."

"What are they doing?" Simon asked.

Henry squinted at the dark shapes in the distance. Someone reached for something—a long, awkward object that was leaning against the house.

"They've got a shovel," Henry said.

"Can you see who it is?" Simon asked.

Henry could only see the three blurry silhouettes, but one was smaller and more slender. "It looks like Mr. Delgado, Officer Myers, and Mrs. Thomas," he said. And then, "Uh-oh. Here they come!"

CHAPTER 18
CONFESSIONS

THE THREE FIGURES were moving toward the front gate of the cemetery. Swiftly, Henry swung his other leg over the top bar of the fence, nearly slicing it open on one of the finials. He perched, off balance, then jumped. He was so worried about being seen by the band of grave robbers that he didn't even think of the long drop to the ground. For a strange, elongated second, he was sailing through the darkening night air, a mosaic of white crosses and headstones mapped out before him. Then he landed on both feet, hard, and tumbled forward on his knees, almost banging his head on a tombstone.

"Hey, good jump," Delilah said, helping him up. Despite his thudding heart, Henry was glad she'd noticed.

"Quick, Hen," Simon whispered. "Get out the map and let's figure out where Julia Thomas's grave is."

Henry took the map from his front shorts pocket and spread it flat against his thigh.

"It's too dark. Turn on the flashlight," Jack said, trying to grab it from Simon.

"Shhh," Simon hushed him. "We can't. They'll see the light."

Delilah knelt on the ground and peered at the map. "We're near this path," she said, tapping the paper with her forefinger. "The one that winds along the back wall. And that's the old section of graves—over there." She stood and pointed. "We have to go this way."

She struck off toward a narrow gravel path, and the boys followed her. "I hope you're right," Simon said. "Because we don't have time to mess around."

Henry stepped softly on the crushed stones, trying not to make a sound. On either side of the path, the tombstones rose in their straight lines, the names of the dead appearing and disappearing in the night, like faint whispers as they walked past.

"Hurry! They're at the gate," Simon said, and in the distance, Henry heard the clank and creak of metal and the low murmur of voices.

"Here!" Delilah whispered urgently. "I found it."

She was a dozen yards ahead, in the section of the graveyard where the tombstones were dark and tilted and the grass grew in renegade clumps. In front of her was the brown tilted tombstone with JULIA ELENA THOMAS in block letters across the top. Henry shivered in recognition. What lay beneath it in the hard earth? Was it the deathbed ore of Jacob Waltz?

Then he froze. Through the black air, he heard a man's voice.

"It's over in that far corner. Follow me."

Whipping around, Henry could just make out the bulky shape of Richard Delgado leading Officer Myers and Julia Thomas down the path, toward the corner of the cemetery where they were crouching. Mr. Delgado carried a shovel, and it looked like Officer Myers was toting a long pole of some sort. In the faint gleam of moonlight, his police badge flashed silver.

"We have to hide!" Simon whispered. He spun, looking in every direction. "These old tombstones are too small. Look—over there!"

He pointed to a massive granite monument about thirty yards away, raised off the ground on a large rectangular slab. Two ornate sculpted urns flanked it.

"We won't be able to see what they're doing from way over there," Jack protested.

"Shhhh!" Henry grabbed his arm. "Come on, Jack. There's no time."

They scrambled off the path into the grass and raced over the graves to the monument. Delilah ran lightly after them, and Simon followed. They squeezed against each other behind the headstone and waited.

Henry pressed his sweaty palms against the cold stone, his breath tight in his lungs. Delilah's shoulder was under his chin and Jack's elbow pressed into his side. The three dark shapes advanced down the path, the large shovel swinging loosely in Mr. Delgado's hand.

"This is a waste of time." Julia Thomas's crisp voice floated toward them. "The real gold is in the gold mine. We should be working on a plan to get that . . . before those kids go back and take it."

"They won't go up the mountain again," Officer Myers replied confidently. "The avalanche scared them. And"—Henry thought his voice sounded conciliatory— "you've done a good job, with that message you wrote in the dirt and the one you put in the girl's bike basket. I don't think we have to worry about them going after the gold. They think it's buried by that rock slide forever."

Henry turned to the others and saw their outraged expressions. "They're confessing to everything," Simon hissed. "I wish we had a tape recorder." Delilah nodded in grim agreement.

"Hey! They wrote the words in the dirt," Jack whispered, and he clenched his fist against Henry's leg.

"Shhhh, Jack, quiet," Simon warned, his words barely audible.

"Your gunshots didn't scare them off," the librarian retorted. They were passing the monument now, approaching the section of old tombstones.

"They tried to KILL you!" Jack whispered to Henry, outraged.

"Down," Simon said softly, and Henry, Jack, and Delilah crouched even lower, in a jumble of knees and elbows.

Mrs. Thomas's sharp voice carried through the thin night air. "And if bullets don't, I can't think what would. They're obsessed with the history of this place."

"Huh," Mr. Delgado snorted. "That's pretty funny coming from you, Julia. You've turned yourself into a copy of a woman who lived a hundred years ago, right down to her name and her handwriting."

Henry turned to Delilah in astonishment. Was this

it? Would they finally learn the explanation for the strange resemblance between the librarian Julia Thomas and her namesake?

Mrs. Thomas brushed him aside. "She was my great-great-aunt! Of course there are family similarities. And Thomas was my middle name already. It wasn't difficult to change that to my last name legally."

Behind the monument, the ripple of surprise was palpable. But in their desperation to keep silent, the boys and Delilah could only stare at each other with widened eyes. Unable to contain herself, Delilah leaned close to Henry's ear and breathed, "No wonder they look so much alike!"

"Julia," Officer Myers was saying, "he's right. You live in the past."

"My knowledge of the past is what's gotten us this far," she snapped. "And it's going to get us the gold. If those kids don't get it first."

Henry peered around the edge of the monument and saw that the librarian and the two men were in the older section of the graveyard now, among the crooked, discolored tombstones, bending over the graves.

"I don't understand how they've been able to figure

out so much, though," Mrs. Thomas continued. "There must have been something at Hank Cormody's place that pointed them to the gold mine. I knew we weren't thorough enough. We should have searched that desk more carefully."

Henry, Simon, and Jack looked at each other in indignation. They'd broken into Uncle Hank's house! And searched it! When Henry thought of them poking around among Uncle Hank's private things, it made his skin crawl.

"No," Officer Myers said sharply. "It would have been too risky. And if anyone besides those kids starts to suspect what we've been up to, you know what it means. We'll all have to leave Superstition for good. We've broken a half-dozen laws already, and we're just lucky I've been able to keep the rest of the police department off our tail."

Through the darkness, Henry thought he saw Mrs. Thomas shrug. "If we find the gold, we'll all be leaving Superstition for good anyway. That's always been the plan."

"Hold on," Mr. Delgado interrupted. "This is it."

Shifting positions, Henry and Simon slowly lifted their heads to spy over the top of the monument.

The three grown-ups were clustered around the tombstone of Julia Elena Thomas. Henry could see that Mr. Delgado was pacing the perimeter of the grave, then pausing to stamp the ground with his boot. "Pass me the pole, Dave, and I'll see where the coffin is located."

"It had better not be a coffin or we'll be digging up Julia's great-great-aunt," Officer Myers said.

"Nonsense," the librarian replied. "My aunt is buried in Phoenix."

"Well, not coffin, then . . . treasure chest!" Mr. Delgado took the pole and repeatedly thrust it into the ground.

Finally, he said, "Here it is! I can feel something. We should dig here."

Officer Myers grabbed the shovel and positioned the blade, pressing it into the ground with his heel. He began lifting shovelfuls of dirt and dumping them to the side in a growing pile, grunting with the effort.

Delilah unfolded herself, half standing next to Henry, her braid brushing his cheek. "What do you think it is?" she whispered.

"I hope not the gold!" Henry said fervently. "Or a dead body . . ."

"Did you hear something?" Mrs. Thomas's voice sliced through the air.

The children immediately ducked to the ground behind the monument and froze. Simon pressed his finger to his lips and shook his head almost imperceptibly at the others.

"No," Officer Myers replied. "You always think you're hearing something."

"And I'm usually right," the librarian said.

"Well, I don't hear anything," Officer Myers retorted, and from behind the massive monument Henry could hear the rhythmic crunch and scrape of the shovel as he resumed digging. Finally, there was a dull *thunk*.

"This is it," Officer Myers said excitedly.

Richard Delgado's voice chimed in, "It looks like some kind of box. Shine the flashlight over here, Julia."

"We have to see," Jack whispered, struggling to raise his head.

"Okay," Simon answered. "But be careful and stay quiet."

The children again untangled themselves and peeked around the edges of the monument. This time they could see all three of the treasure hunters gathered around the lip of the hole that Officer Myers had dug. Now Richard Delgado was using the shovel to pry something loose from the dry ground.

"I've got it," he said, panting. "Try to pull it out now."

Officer Myers and Julia Thomas bent over the hole, arms extended, tugging and straining. They managed to lift something dark and rectangular. Henry saw it was a small wooden box that they struggled with . . . as if the earth were pulling it in the opposite direction, reluctant to let go. Finally, they placed it on the ground next to the hole.

"See?" Richard Delgado said triumphantly. "It's not a coffin. It's a chest."

"It's locked," Mrs. Thomas said, her voice high with excitement.

"Stand back," Officer Myers ordered. Henry watched, breathless, as the policeman took his gun from the holster and aimed it at the padlock on the box.

Jack nudged Henry. "He's going to SHOOT it!" he whispered, just as the cemetery's stillness was shattered by the loud crack of a gunshot.

The children all dropped to their stomachs in terror. *What if he hears us,* Henry was thinking, *and turns that thing on us?*

"Great!" Mr. Delgado exclaimed. "Let's open it."

Delilah and the boys scrambled back to their feet, peering over the top of the monument.

"Allow me," Julia Thomas said. "It *is* my aunt's grave site." She knelt next to the box and slowly lifted the lid.

CHAPTER 19
PRECIOUS BEQUEST

WHAT CAME NEXT happened so quickly that Henry could hardly make sense of it.

The lid of the old box creaked open, and the tense anticipation among the three grown-ups suddenly shifted.

"What?" Mr. Delgado said.

"Ugh," Officer Myers grunted.

Mrs. Thomas gave a cry of exasperation. "It's nothing but a bunch of bones." In the blurry darkness, Henry could see her lean over the box with the flashlight. "They look like animal bones."

But as she was saying this, something fast and black and furious—a whizzing ball of fur and claws—sailed through the air and landed in the open box.

At first, Henry couldn't understand what was happening. But then he saw a telltale patch of white.

"Oh!" he gasped. "It's JOSIE!" He felt himself pitching forward, around the side of the monument, instinctively rushing to save her from the grave robbers. But before he could, Simon grabbed his shirt and held him back.

"No, Hen," he whispered.

Josie was in the box, her body fully covering whatever lay inside it, her fur raised, her ears flat against her skull, and her wrath-filled golden eyes glowing in the darkness. She yowled and spat, striking at Mrs. Thomas's outstretched hand.

"Ouch!" Mrs. Thomas screamed, jumping back. "It's that cat again, the same one!" She turned to Officer Myers. "It's vicious. Shoot it."

Henry's heart seized. Now all the children scrambled to their feet—*Josie? Shoot Josie?*—but before they could do anything, Officer Myers said, "Don't be ridiculous. It's just a stray. I don't know why it doesn't like you, but I'm certainly not going to kill it for that."

Henry was trembling with panic. What if the policeman changed his mind? They wouldn't be able to reach Josie in time to save her. Simon motioned for the others to crouch down behind the monument again, and Henry reluctantly ducked.

Delilah turned to Henry, her eyes huge. "What is Josie doing there? Did she follow us?"

Henry shook his head in wonderment. "I don't know. I didn't see her. There's something about Mrs. Thomas that she just hates. It's the same way she reacted at the library, remember?"

"But then why did she come here?" Delilah asked.

"We need to see what's in the box," Simon whispered.

"That creepy librarian wanted to kill Josie!" Jack whispered, his eyes huge.

Near the open grave, Mrs. Thomas recoiled in disgust, rising from her knees while Josie continued to yowl and hiss at her. She brushed off her trousers and said coldly, "Then we're done here. Richard, you can clean up this mess in the morning."

"Animal bones!" Mr. Delgado said. "I don't get it. Why would someone bury an animal in a grave marked with the name of a person? Do you think this was a pet?"

Henry felt an icy realization prickle beneath his skin. *A pet.*

"Who knows?" Officer Myers replied. "And who cares? It's not what we're looking for."

Julia Thomas backed away from Josie's enraged, hunched form. "I told you we should be focusing on the mine," she said. "We need to figure out how to get our hands on that gold."

Still grumbling over their disappointment, the librarian and the two men collected their tools and strode out of the cemetery, while Henry, Simon, Jack, and Delilah huddled behind the monument, too frightened to budge.

As soon as they heard the wrought-iron gate clank shut, they got up from their hiding spot and quietly crossed the grassy distance to the open grave. Henry could see the backs of the three adults receding toward the house and hear the fading murmur of their voices.

"Keep your voices down," Simon cautioned, leading the way. "Let's see what got Josie so riled up."

A small, splintered wooden box, dark with dirt, was sitting on the ground. Its lid was toppled to the side. Josie huddled inside it, filling it, her body covering whatever it contained.

"Josie," Simon said. "Here, Josie." He snapped his fingers. She lifted her head and stared at them. Henry noticed that her fur was smooth again, but her ears were still flat against her head, signaling her distemper.

"Why won't she move?"

"I think she's protecting it," Henry said.

"I'll pick her up," Jack said. He reached down and grabbed Josie, hoisting her in the air, at which point she turned rigid, hissing and spitting, trying to break free. Jack held her fast.

With a quick glance in the direction of the caretaker's house—which looked quiet, its door closed—Simon clicked on his flashlight. An assemblage of delicate bones flashed whitely in the dark contours of the box. Henry saw a small, elongated skull at one end. He shivered, watching as Josie tried to lunge toward the box again.

"What is wrong with her?" Jack complained, clamping her against his chest.

"It's an animal," Simon said slowly.

"It's a cat," Henry corrected him. "The black cat from the saloon. Julia Thomas's cat."

"The one from the picture, that looks like Josie?" Jack asked. "How do you know?"

"Because I know," Henry said, and he saw Delilah's stricken face in the soft glow of the flashlight.

"That's why Josie is so upset," Delilah said. "And why she hates the librarian . . . who's trying to act like the real Julia Thomas, but isn't. Josie can tell."

"Oh, come on," Simon said. "She's a cat. How can she tell that?"

"Because there's a connection, Simon," Henry said desperately. "This proves it! Josie is Julia Thomas's cat, reincarnated." He reached for Josie, who was still struggling and hissing in Jack's arms. "It's okay, Josie," he said as he held her, stroking the silky top of her head. "We'll put it back in the ground."

Delilah knelt and swiftly settled the lid over the skeleton, thumping it down with her palms. Just as abruptly, Henry felt Josie relax. Her ears twitched.

"Wait a second," Simon said. "Even if what you say is true, even if Josie is some kind of . . . reincarnated cat from the 1800s, we can't close up the box and bury it again. Then they'll know we were here. We have to leave things just the way they were."

"No," Delilah said. She was already dragging the wooden box back toward the hole. "It's a grave! No one should ever have touched it."

"She's right," Henry agreed. "We should put the box back, even if it makes Mr. Delgado suspect something tomorrow morning."

"Even *if* it makes him suspect something?" Simon held up his hands in exasperation. "Of course he'll suspect something! Delilah, stop." He stomped his foot in front of the box, blocking its path.

Delilah whirled around, and despite the darkness, Henry could see her eyes flashing. "You cut that out!" she said. "I'm putting it back!"

"No, you're not," Simon said sharply. "That's insane.

If we were going to do this, we might as well not even have bothered to hide! We should have announced we were here and helped them."

"I would not have helped them," Jack said staunchly, missing the point. "They are the bad guys. And Josie doesn't like them."

Josie slipped free of Henry's grasp and slunk noiselessly into the shadows, where she sat watching them.

Delilah bent over, tugging on the box. Simon planted his foot on top of it, holding it still.

"Argh! Let it go!" Delilah protested.

"You're making too much noise," Simon said. "They'll hear you. Is that what you want? Do you want them to catch us?"

"No, she doesn't." Henry intervened. "But we have to bury the box. A grave is"—he hesitated, searching for the right word—"*sanctified*."

"What does that mean?" Jack demanded.

"Holy," Henry said. "Sacred ground that shouldn't be disturbed."

Jack looked around nervously. "Does that mean the ghosts might get mad?"

Simon groaned. "There's no such thing as ghosts."

He turned to Henry beseechingly. "Hen, it's the grave for a *cat*," he said, but Henry could feel him giving up.

With a final ferocious pull, Delilah yanked the box out from under Simon's foot and toppled it back into the open grave, where it landed with a thud.

"There!" she said, standing. She brushed her hands off. "Now let's put the dirt back."

"This is crazy," Simon muttered in resignation. "They'll know we were here."

"Well, they don't scare *me*!" Jack declared. "Nothing scares me"—he frowned—"except that curse." He turned to Henry. "Promise me we'll put my gold back! We have to do it SOON."

"We will, Jack," Henry said. "I promise." In the faint moonlight, he could see the dark mass of Superstition Mountain far across the desert. They were destined to go back, Henry decided. The question was, were they destined to return home?

Cupping their hands, they scooped the loose earth from the pile and covered the box. Then they used their sneakers to kick the rest of the dirt into the hole.

On the edge of the grave site, Josie sat as still as a statue, only her tail twitching. She watched until the last clump of dirt had filled the grave, then turned and darted off into the night.

Delilah crouched and patiently patted it down, smoothing the surface.

"There," she said. "That's better." She sat back on her heels and stared at the dark, crumbling tombstone at one end of the grave. "Huh," she said. "Simon, shine the flashlight over here."

Simon directed the beam over the tombstone, where they could read the faded block letters JULIA ELENA THOMAS across the rough face. "What's the matter?"

Delilah pointed to the dates at the bottom of the stone. "I thought it said 1825 the last time we were here, but it says 1875, doesn't it? 1875 to 1896. So that could be the lifespan of a cat."

"Twenty-one years? That seems really long," Simon said skeptically.

"Well, they're supposed to have nine lives," Henry said. "I hope Josie lives that long."

"Where did Josie go?" Jack asked.

"She's probably home already," Simon said. He swung the flashlight over the ghostly landscape of tombstones, pale in the moonlight.

Then they saw her.

She was only a few yards away, stretched across the top of a headstone. Her body looked calm and relaxed, in stark contrast to her furious pose earlier. One paw hung down, over the face of the stone where a name was etched in large block letters.

Henry stiffened. "Hey," he said. "Isn't that . . ."

Delilah stood and gently touched his arm.

Without saying a word, Simon directed the beam over the letters they all knew would be there.

CHAPTER 20
THE GOLD MINE BECKONS

B<small>ARKER</small>.

There beneath the arc of white light: the familiar letters of their name, etched in the stone.

They walked slowly toward the grave. Josie pricked her ears, watching them steadily, her tail curled in a question mark.

There was still something so shocking about it: their name—their mother and father's name!—written on a tombstone here in this desolate place, in the middle of the desert.

"At least it doesn't have dates," Delilah said. "That would be really creepy."

"If there were dates, we would know the grave was for someone else," Henry contradicted.

Simon shook his head. "It *is* for someone else, Hen.

Calm down." He shone the flashlight over the granite face, illuminating each letter. "You know what's strange?" he said. "This one isn't old like the others. Look at the stone."

Henry saw what he meant. Though it was composed of thin, light lines, the inscription was crisp. The granite was smooth and clear, not pocked and stained like the other headstones in the area. A tombstone that said BARKER, that was new, with no dates . . . it was beginning to seem worse and worse! But just as his heart was pounding so hard he thought it would burst from his chest, Henry realized something.

"Wait," he said. He shoved his hand in his pocket, scrabbling his fingers till they grazed the folded cemetery map. "I think . . ." He pulled out the creased paper and shook it open. "Shine the light over here, Simon," he said urgently. "Look at the map. I think this is where . . ."

"It's Uncle Hank's plot!" Simon understood instantly. He grabbed the map from Henry and flattened it against the tombstone. "Here's the grave of Julia Thomas," he said, jabbing one of Henry's ballpoint circles and shifting the orientation of the paper. "So that means . . ."

Delilah shouldered next to him. "There are three graves in between. Here, here, and here."

"Look," Henry cried. "Those are the three graves in between, and that means this must be Uncle Hank's plot."

"We found it!" Jack shouted jubilantly.

"SHHHHHHH," the others hushed him.

All the excitement disturbed Josie, who leapt from her perch and streaked off into the night.

Frowning, Simon directed the flashlight back at the tombstone emblazoned with BARKER. "Uncle Hank bought a cemetery plot when he planned to be cremated. He even bought a tombstone. And he put our last name on it. It doesn't make sense."

"Unless . . . ," Henry said slowly. "Unless he did it for us. Maybe he left us something here."

Simon was nodding in the darkness. "And this was how he planned for us to find it. It had to be something he couldn't leave in his will. Or something he thought somebody might try to steal before we got here. So he buried it in his cemetery plot and put our last name on the tombstone."

"But why would he expect you guys to come to the cemetery?" Delilah asked. "Once you knew he was cremated, you would never think to look for a grave."

"Because of the note he left for me," Henry said. "He

said our name would outlast death, and here it is." He gestured at the tombstone, noticing again the strange finality of their name in the granite.

"Well, we came to the cemetery before we found that note," Simon amended. " 'Cuz it's an interesting place to look around."

"Yeah," Jack agreed.

They stood in a small shrouded semicircle around the grave, with the pale tombstones unfurling on all sides.

"I don't want to dig up any more graves," Delilah said.

Henry looked at her pinched forehead and wondered how she felt, standing here in the graveyard, when she, more than any of them, knew what death really was.

Simon, however, was undaunted by her protest. "It's not a grave," he told her.

"Yeah," Jack declared. "It might have buried TREA-SURE in it!"

"That's what you thought about the other grave," Delilah said, unfazed. "And it had a dead cat in it."

"The other Josie," Jack added.

"No, Jack." Exasperated, Simon glanced at his watch. "It's nine o'clock. We should get going."

Henry turned to him in surprise. Only nine o'clock?

It felt like they had been in the cemetery for hours. With the sliver of moon in the night sky, the stark rows of gravestones, and the pulsing silence, it could have been past midnight.

"We're just going to leave it here?" he asked, shocked.

"The grave?" Simon snorted. "Uh, yeah. It's not like we can take it with us. And we didn't bring a shovel to dig it up." He cast a quick glance at Delilah. "But I think you're right, Hen. He left something for us here." Henry thought of Uncle Hank buying the plot, having a granite stone carved with their last name, and then writing the note for Henry to read after he died. What had he buried there? Was it the gold he had been searching for? The deathbed ore of Jacob Waltz?

Simon swung the flashlight in the direction of the length of fence they'd climbed. "Follow me," he said. "We'll have to boost each other over."

They all trailed after him, stepping softly over and around the grassy graves until they reached the path. The night air had turned chilly, and the distant rustlings of desert animals reverberated in the silence. What was out there? Henry wondered.

"This is a good place for ghosts," Jack whispered, glancing around.

Henry kept his eyes on the path. He couldn't bear to look at the faces of the tombstones, as he marched silently alongside them. He was afraid he might see other names he recognized.

Then they had reached the fence. Beyond its spiked railing, Henry could barely discern the blackness of Superstition Mountain, a blurred mystery. They would be back there soon enough. He sensed that it was waiting for them.

After a rushed good-bye to Delilah at the end of her street, the boys pedaled furiously back home, swinging their bikes into the driveway just as their father was carrying the recycling bin out to the street.

"There you are!" he exclaimed. "Your mother just called Delilah's house looking for you."

"We rode out by the cemetery," Simon told him promptly.

"At night?" Mr. Barker raised his eyebrows. "That sounds spooky."

"It was!" Jack declared. "But we didn't see any ghosts," he added, disappointed.

"Oh well," Mr. Barker said. "Maybe next time."

Mrs. Barker was less understanding. "It's almost nine

thirty!" she scolded. "If you can't make it home by nine o'clock, we'll have to make your curfew earlier."

As with many parental edicts, this made little sense to Henry. If they couldn't make it home by nine, it seemed obvious that their curfew should be LATER, not earlier. But the parental mind was a contrary thing and did not often work logically.

"Okay, okay," Simon said. "Sorry! We were riding around and lost track of time."

"I don't like you riding your bikes so late at night, either," Mrs. Barker said, piling on admonishments. "You could get hit by a car."

"We were out by the cemetery," Simon assured her. "There weren't any cars."

"That's even worse. What if something had happened to one of you? How would you have gotten help?"

There was no winning, Henry decided as his mother herded them down the hallway to their bedrooms.

Minutes later, they crowded around the bathroom sink, finally alone.

"So when are we going back to the cemetery to dig up the grave?" Simon asked. "Tomorrow?"

"No!" Jack protested. "We have to take the gold back first! Before I die," he added glumly.

Simon rolled his eyes. "Jack, listen. It's been weeks since you took the gold, and you've been fine. I'm pretty sure a couple more days won't matter."

"You're not the one with the curse on you," Jack grumbled.

"Neither are you!" Simon exploded. "Come on. Don't you want to find out what's buried in ol' Uncle Hank's grave? What if it's money? Or jewels? Or gold we can actually keep?" Simon's eyes lit up and he rubbed his hands together. "We could be RICH. Legit rich! And it'll be so easy, 'cuz we won't have to worry about how to get the gold off the mountain."

"Well . . ." Henry hesitated. "Delilah's right. The last time we thought that, it was a coffin with a dead cat in it."

"Which just means that Jacob Waltz's gold is somewhere else!" Simon said. "And we could be the ones to find it."

"You don't care if I DIE," Jack protested, enraged. "All you care about is getting rich." He balled up his fist and slugged Simon in the arm.

"Owww!" Simon yelped. He whipped around and grabbed Jack's shoulders, thumping him against the closed bathroom door.

"Hey, stop!" Henry whispered urgently, wedging himself between them. "Or Mom will come back here and wonder what's going on."

As Jack continued to swing his fists in Simon's direction, Henry tried to reason with Simon. "Come on, Simon. We both promised him we'd take the gold back to the mine on Sunday. Remember? When Mom and Dad go to the art museum with Aunt Kathy and Emmett."

"But that's two whole days away!" Simon protested. "I don't want to wait that long to go back to see what's in Uncle Hank's grave."

"I know," Henry said. "But it'd be hard to go to the cemetery before then. We can't go during the day or someone might see us digging up the grave. And Mom and Dad won't let us stay out so late at night again. Plus, when Mr. Delgado sees that Julia Thomas's grave is all filled in, he's going to be suspicious . . . so we should stay away for a while."

Aggravated, Simon clawed his hand through his hair. "I told you we shouldn't have put the box back!"

Henry shrugged. "Well, it's too late to change that. So we might as well go up the mountain and return the gold. Right?"

Simon sighed. "Yeah, I guess."

"Yeah," Jack added, kicking Simon in the shin for good measure. Simon glared at him, but their mother knocked on the door before he could retaliate.

"Boys, hurry up! It's time for bed."

Docilely, they filed out of the bathroom and headed toward their separate bedrooms. As Henry crawled inside the cool sheets, his mind was racing. He opened the drawer of his nightstand and felt around for Uncle Hank's note.

In the dim glow of the nightlight he read again the words that his great-uncle had written to him before he died:

Dear Henry,

Your name is my name. It will outlast death—the way a place can be about death but outlast death. If you believe that, you'll know where to find something I left for you and your brothers. Live well, Henry.

Love, Uncle Hank

Carefully, he folded the note and returned it to the drawer. *Live well, Henry.* Was it a wish? Or an order?

CHAPTER 21

RETURN TO SUPERSTITION MOUNTAIN

IT TOOK NO SMALL AMOUNT of persuasion on the boys' part to get their parents to let them stay home while Mr. and Mrs. Barker, Aunt Kathy, and Emmett drove into Phoenix to spend the day at the art museum. Mrs. Barker had been looking forward to a family outing all week; Mr. Barker wanted the boys along so that he would have an audience for his funny comments about modern art. But when Simon promised that they would clean up the garage, Henry could tell they were both wavering. Since their move to Uncle Hank's house at the beginning of the summer, the garage had remained the last frontier of disorder. Moving boxes were piled high against the rear wall, some of them partially and messily unpacked, some of them still taped shut. The garage was Mr. Barker's domain, so Mrs. Barker left it alone. Since Mr. Barker had no interest or investment in any particular system of organization, it was the one area of the house where the boys were given free rein.

"Like goes with like," Mr. Barker advised. "That's all I ask."

"What does that mean?" Jack asked. "We put the things that we like together?"

Henry had a brief vision of the jai alai set being grouped with the hammer, because Jack was fond of both of those. "No, Jack," Henry said. "It means we put things that are"—he struggled for the right word—"*homogeneous* together."

Mr. Barker laughed, ruffling Henry's curls. "Exactly! Homogeneous, not hodgepodgeneous. Think you can handle that?"

"Sure," Simon said expansively. "Leave it to us! It's going to look great."

"Well"—Mrs. Barker sighed—"I would be thrilled to have the garage in order. But I do wish we could all go to the museum together! I feel like we've spent the whole summer moving into this house. I wanted us to have some fun."

Henry marveled that his mother's perception of the summer could be so different from his own. All they'd done was *move in*? Moving in had been the least of the summer's preoccupations! They'd climbed Superstition Mountain three times already. They'd discovered a long-lost gold mine. They'd uncovered a curse and a conspiracy and Uncle Hank's true love. It suddenly occurred to Henry that he and his parents lived parallel lives, running similar courses but never quite intersecting . . . in the same place, with the same props, but filled with vastly different experiences.

"We should be back by five o'clock," Mrs. Barker said. "Please be careful unpacking the boxes! Some of them are heavy."

"We will," the boys chorused, trying not to appear too eager for their parents to leave.

Delilah showed up right on schedule, and for the next two hours they all worked feverishly to put the garage in order. Jack was in charge of opening and emptying boxes, a job he performed noisily and with gusto, ripping the packing tape, emptying the contents onto the garage floor, and then crushing the cardboard cartons and stacking them. Henry sorted the garden spades, tennis rackets, rakes, and hoses into their correct groups, and Delilah arranged them on the garage shelves and against the walls. Simon's sole responsibility was their father's tool bench, where he planted himself to create some kind of order out of the stupefying array of wrenches, bolts, and drill bits.

"Keep up the pace!" he commanded periodically. "We need to start up the mountain by eleven. It's going to be really hot."

"I got extra water," Delilah said.

"Yeah, so did I."

Henry could see Simon's black backpack and Delilah's pink one leaning against the side of the house, filled with the necessary provisions for their climb, along with a garden spade, rope, and flashlight. He was thirsty already, soaked in sweat, and covered in a light film of grime from the unpacking. But they were almost finished. Out on the driveway, Jack was crushing the last moving box, jumping vigorously on the cardboard.

"I'll sweep," Henry offered. "Then we can go." He took the large janitor's broom and pushed it back and forth across the concrete floor, clearing the dust and debris.

"Hey, this looks really good!" Jack declared in surprise. "We did a GREAT job!"

Henry had to admit the garage was transformed. The moving boxes were gone. The walls and shelves were as orderly as a hardware store's. Mr. Barker's bench full of tools in their cubbies and cases gleamed with possibility, and the floor was swept clean.

"Mom will be happy," he said. "And it didn't even take us that long."

"That's because I helped," Delilah said nonchalantly.

Normally, Henry might have minded her smugness. But he was beginning to realize that when Delilah bragged about one of her skills or personality traits, she tended to be right . . . and that made it seem less like bragging and more like an observation of fact.

In a matter of minutes, they washed off their faces and hands, used the bathroom, took big swigs of water at the kitchen sink, and slathered themselves with sun lotion, filling the house with a pungent odor of mango and coconut. Jack had put his collection of gold flakes in a clear plastic sandwich bag, which he now held up to the sunlight pouring through the sliding glass doors. The gold flashed and sparkled.

He sighed. "I wish we didn't have to take them back," he said morosely.

"Oh, SHEESH, Jack," Simon snapped. "All you've been saying for days is that we had to take them back to the gold mine as soon as possible! Make up your mind."

Jack's face clouded. "I said that 'cuz I don't want to be DEAD," he groused. "But I still wish I could keep my gold."

Henry put his arm around Jack's shoulders. "The important thing is that you found the gold mine," he said. "That's what really matters. Even without the gold, you'll always know you did that."

"I guess," Jack mumbled. "But I want to keep my gold."

He was still complaining about it as they grabbed the backpacks and began their journey through the foothills toward the craggy wilderness of Superstition Mountain.

The first part of the climb was so familiar to Henry that it passed quickly—a blur of shrubbery and spiked grasses, the occasional stately cactus, the vivid pockets of purple and yellow wildflowers. As the ground became rockier and steeper, he noticed the remnants of their past exploration: a few of the sticks Simon had propped in the sand to mark the path the very first time they'd ascended the mountain, back in June. After a while, he turned around and saw the roofs of the houses in their neighborhood dwindling to insignificance, like the tiny green roofs of the houses in the board game Monopoly, which he and his brothers sometimes played. The mountain began to assert itself, stern in its silence.

"It almost looks like it might rain," Delilah said once, stopping to rest for a minute against a boulder. The sun was a blazing sphere high above them, but the sky had a strange layering of clouds that periodically muted the light.

"Yeah," Simon agreed. "I don't think it's rained since we got here. Has it?"

Henry couldn't remember it raining over the summer. He thought of the heavy summer rains in Chicago and the lush greenery of their old backyard. It was so dry here, a place constitutionally opposed to water.

They kept climbing. Occasionally a small brown lizard flitted out from under a bush and studied them with its bright eyes. The only sounds were the chattering of birds, the crunch of their feet on the rocks, and their noisy breathing as the slope became steeper. Even Jack was quiet from the exertion.

Henry walked behind Delilah, thinking about their last trip up the mountain, when she'd struggled to keep up with all of them, her leg in a cast.

"Does your leg hurt at all?" he asked her.

"Nope!" she said, smiling back at him. "It'll be much easier and faster for me to climb down into the canyon. Maybe I can even look for my dad's compass."

Henry remembered so vividly the moment when the compass had slipped from her grasp and she had lunged after it, tumbling down the canyon wall and breaking her leg.

"I really hope we find it," he said.

"Yeah, me too. But I kind of doubt we will. An animal could have taken it by now, or it could be buried under something."

Henry was surprised at how cheerful she sounded. "You don't seem so . . . worried about it anymore," he said, watching her.

Delilah sighed. "Well, I would still really like to find it, 'cuz it was my dad's. All the things that were his, when I touch them, I think of his hands touching them . . . you know?"

Henry nodded. It was how he felt when he held the letter that Uncle Hank had written to him, the sense of his great-uncle's spirit flowing through the paper and into his hands.

"But then," Delilah continued, "I thought that my dad wouldn't want me to be upset about losing the compass. He would say, 'It's just a thing, it doesn't matter.' Things don't matter as much as people do."

"No," Henry agreed. "But they're a way of remembering people."

Delilah nodded. "That's why it would be great to find it. But I don't *need* to find it anymore, the way I did at the beginning of the summer."

Henry smiled at her. "That's good."

"Hey," Delilah said suddenly, stopping.

"What?" Henry almost bumped into her.

"Did you see that?"

"What?"

Delilah frowned, squinting into the patchwork of bushes and boulders. "I thought I saw something."

Henry followed her gaze into the thickets of gray-green vegetation along the path. "Maybe it was a bird?"

Delilah shook her head. "Something bigger than that."

A little ahead of them, Simon stopped too, unzipping his backpack. "Let's take a water break," he suggested.

"Yeah, I'm thirsty!" Jack snatched a bottle of water from Simon's pack.

They gathered around a large reddish rock, unscrewing the caps of their water bottles and dousing their parched mouths. The water was still cool from the kitchen tap, and as it poured over Henry's lips and into the collar of his shirt, he marveled that something so ordinary could taste so good.

Delilah continued to scrutinize the bushes uneasily.

"What's the matter?" Simon asked her.

She twisted her braid in one hand. "I think some-one's following us."

Henry turned to her in surprise. "You mean Officer Myers and the others?"

Simon came to stand beside her, scanning the dense shrubbery on the side of the trail. "Did you see someone?"

"I saw some*thing*," Delilah said. "In the bushes. And . . ." She hesitated. "I can feel it."

Henry looked around, at the prickly cactuses and

red-brown boulders and stunted trees. The mountain's heavy stillness, its tense waiting quality, was utterly recognizable to him now.

Jack shrugged. "It always feels creepy up here."

"It's more than that," Delilah said, her eyes darting over the landscape.

"I checked to make sure nobody was following us when we left home," Simon said. "But they've done that before and we didn't see them. So, okay, we'll keep an eye out. We're almost to the canyon anyway."

Delilah held on to her water bottle, but they put the others away. Henry and Simon took the backpacks, hoisting them on their shoulders as they resumed climbing.

They had gone only a short distance when Delilah grabbed Henry's arm.

"Look!" she whispered, clutching her water bottle against her chest. "Over there."

CHAPTER 22

"SOMEONE IS WATCHING US . . ."

DELILAH POINTED into the brambly undergrowth. This time, Henry did see something—a shadow of movement, dappled by sunlight. And he felt it now too: the mysterious weight of someone's gaze on him. Despite the heat, he shivered.

"Simon," he said softly. "We're being followed."

Simon dropped his backpack in the dirt and walked over to the edge of the trail. "Who's there?" he shouted.

This was a bold move, Henry thought. What were they going to do if somebody answered? Especially if it was Officer Myers, with his gun?

But the woods were silent. "I can feel it. Someone is watching us," Delilah said, turning to Henry.

"I know," Henry said. A thin electric tension pulsed

through the air. It was more than the strange atmosphere of the mountain; it felt closer and more personal.

"Keep going," Simon said grimly. "The sooner we get to the mine, the sooner we can go home." He led the way, glancing over his shoulder at the wilderness along the trail.

Henry saw that they were coming to the high boulders that rimmed the canyon, where Jack had fallen so many weeks ago, and where they'd found the three skulls.

Then, just as they rounded the bend, he saw it: a flash of movement, tawny in the sunlight, darting through the trees on the other side of the trail. And in an instant—even before it appeared above them, crouched on a high pile of boulders—he knew what it was.

A mountain lion.

"Oh!" Delilah gasped. Simon, ahead of them, stopped in his tracks, and Jack, who had been charging along, crashed into him and yelped in surprise.

On the bluff, the mountain lion watched them, its ears pricked. A low growl rumbled from its chest. It was so big, Henry thought—a rippling honey-colored mass of muscle. The fierce black markings on its face looked like

war paint. Its thick tail waved above its haunches. Deep in their dark rims, its golden eyes stared intently, watching them.

Despite the wave of fear that paralyzed him, Henry felt an unexpected thrill. The mountain lion was so *wild*. And so close. The gap of a few yards seemed like nothing between them. And the mountain, the lion, the sun-dappled landscape, this moment frozen in time—everything felt, suddenly, so *alive*.

"It's been *stalking* us," Henry whispered, awed.

Simon didn't take his eyes off the mountain lion. He said in a loud voice, "Stand as tall as possible. Start stamping your feet."

"What?" Henry said. "Won't that make it mad?"

"No," Simon shouted, already thudding his feet on the ground.

Stamp, stomp, stamp, stomp, stamp, stomp!

"We have to be loud and BIG," he yelled. "It's the only thing that works with mountain lions."

How does he know that? Henry wondered. *And what if he's wrong?*

But Simon had already hoisted his backpack high on his shoulders and was shouting, "GO AWAY!!!"

Jack gamely joined him, pounding his feet in the dust

and yelling at the top of his lungs, "Go away, you big lion, you! We're not scared of you!"

The mountain lion's ears twitched, and Henry thought he saw it shift its position on the boulder.

He grabbed a branch from the side of the trail and beat it fiercely against the bushes. "YAHHHHHH!" he yelled.

Delilah looked at them like they were crazy.

"Come on," Simon told her. "Make a lot of noise."

"Okay," she said. She unscrewed the cap of her water bottle and hurled the half-full plastic bottle against the rock, where it hit with a crack like a gunshot, sending a spray of water through the air.

The mountain lion's ears flattened. For a fleeting moment, it looked exactly like Josie: thoroughly disgusted with them. Then, as suddenly as it had appeared, it turned and crossed the boulder, leaping into the brush and streaking off through the woods.

Henry collapsed to the ground, his legs trembling with fear and relief.

"Woooo hoooooooo!" Simon yelled, waving his fist in the air. "I can't believe that worked!"

"What do you mean?" Delilah asked. "I thought you said that was the only thing that *would* work."

"Well, that's true. You can't run away or roll into a

ball, 'cuz they'll think you're prey and attack you. The only thing that works is to look like a bigger animal that might attack them. You have to challenge them. But . . ."

"But what?" Henry was still sitting in the dirt, trying to quell his shaking limbs.

"But if that didn't work, the mountain lion would definitely have attacked us. 'Cuz we were provoking it."

"Now you tell us," Delilah said.

"It doesn't matter," Simon crowed. "It worked."

"We saw a MOUNTAIN LION!" Jack cried, dancing around in the dust. "And WE SCARED IT!"

Henry rose unsteadily to his feet. Maybe this was the secret to courage . . . just acting braver all the time than you really felt. Maybe just trying to appear brave, even if you were scared out of your wits, would make you brave—sort of the way that smiling even when you were sad was supposed to make you feel happier. And even if it didn't make you brave, what did it matter? If you did the brave thing, over and over again, while your deepest cowardly heart was quaking with fear, weren't you still, for all intents and purposes, brave?

Well, Henry thought, *I may not be as brave as Uncle Hank, but I can* act *brave. And I just did.*

CHAPTER 23
THE THUNDER GOD SPEAKS

STILL TALKING ABOUT the mountain lion, they climbed the last stretch to the rim of the canyon.

"That was amazing," Henry said.

"I knew there were mountain lions up here!" Jack was exultant. "Rattlesnakes and mountain lions! We saw BOTH of them."

Henry glanced at him dubiously. He hadn't realized there was a checklist of dangers for them to cross off.

"And I knew we were being followed," Delilah said. "You should have listened to me."

"We did listen to you," Simon said. "But you thought it was a person. And anyway, there was nothing we could do until it showed itself."

"That was FUN making so much noise," Jack continued. "I want to do that again."

"I hope we won't have to," Delilah countered.

"Throwing your water bottle was smart," Simon told her. "I think the water and the noise of that were what finally scared the mountain lion away."

"Thanks," Delilah said smugly, smiling at him.

Henry felt a prick of annoyance. "But now you don't have any water left," he said, a little meanly.

"She can share mine," Simon said, as Delilah joined him in the lead on the trail.

Henry trotted glumly after them, as they emerged from the border of trees onto the lip of the canyon.

It opened out below them, the rough walls plummeting to the narrow strip of ground below. And as Henry stood on the edge of rock and surveyed the scene, he saw not a place but a series of summer adventures. There was the ledge where they'd found the three skulls. There was the dry creek bed where Henry had found the bones and the saddlebag. There was the spot where Delilah had fallen, breaking her leg. There was the bush where they'd hidden the saddlebag and where they'd heard the gunshot. And over there, behind the jumble of boulders, was the entrance to the secret canyon.

This wild, strange place was now full of memory and

meaning. With a start, Henry realized that Superstition Mountain was becoming a part of him.

"Okay," Simon said. "We have to keep moving. We don't have much time to get to the gold mine. I'll go first."

"No, let me this time," Delilah said, stepping ahead of him, and starting to lower herself over the rocks.

"You don't get to go first!" Jack exclaimed, horrified. "I want to. It's my turn."

Delilah looked up at him. "Please, Jack? It's going to be so much easier for me this time, without my cast."

Jack wavered, then relented. "Okay," he said grudgingly. "But I get to be first when we climb back up."

When we climb back up sounded so optimistic, Henry thought. He wondered what would happen to them between now and then.

"Sure," Delilah agreed. "That's fair."

And so, with Delilah in the lead, they began their descent, carefully picking their way down the canyon wall.

When they reached the floor of the canyon, they were drenched in sweat, and the reddish brown dust from the climb had darkened the creases in their skin.

"I'm thirsty. And hungry," Jack whined, plopping down in the dirt.

"Okay," Simon said, magnanimous. "We can take another break." He crouched and began unzipping his backpack, removing the water bottles.

Henry went over to sit by Jack, who had a worried look on his face.

"What's the matter?" he asked.

Jack was silent, stubbing his sneakers in the pebbly ground.

"Tell me," Henry coaxed.

"What if that mountain lion was chasing ME? What if that was the curse, 'cuz I took the gold? Maybe he was trying to kill me."

Henry considered this. "He didn't seem to be after you *specifically*," he said.

"Nah," Simon chimed in. "He would have attacked all of us." He thought for a minute. "Actually, they usually go for the smallest, weakest one in the group. That's not you. He probably would have picked Henry or Delilah."

Henry glowered at him, and Delilah looked cross. "I was the one who scared him away!" she protested. "With my water bottle. I am definitely not the weakest one."

Henry did not like where the conversation was headed. "Neither am I," he said hotly.

Jack, however, seemed immensely relieved. He chugged a bottle of water and grabbed one of the chocolate bars that Delilah had brought, already soft from the heat.

"Okay, let's go!" he shouted, revitalized. "Let's put back my gold."

"Yes," Simon agreed. "We should keep moving. The sky looks weird."

Henry glanced at the vast expanse overhead and saw that he was right. The strange layering of clouds had thickened, and the light had turned sharp.

Together, they hurried to the passageway that led to the smaller, secret canyon.

Henry led the way through the narrow chute, his shoulders brushing against the hard rock walls. It would be difficult for the historical society treasure hunters to squeeze through here, he thought. Then again, maybe there was another way into the canyon that they hadn't discovered yet.

As soon as they emerged into the smaller canyon, Henry felt a change in the air. It had turned cooler suddenly, and the sky overhead had darkened. A gust of wind blew, startling him. Rising before them, he saw the enormous face of the rock horse. The stillness of the canyon seemed as tense as a coiled spring.

Simon's forehead wrinkled with worry. "It's going to storm."

As if in answer, a clap of thunder shattered the quiet. *Boom!*

"Jack, hurry," Delilah urged, but Jack, with his fist clenched around the plastic sandwich bag of tiny gold flakes, was already running ahead, the dry dust following him in clouds.

Beneath the fierce sky, the others ran after him, past the rock horse, toward the curtain of rock that hid the entrance to the Lost Dutchman's Mine. Now, because of the avalanche, it was a massive drift of boulders. Shuddering, Henry remembered the crashing sound of the rocks pouring down the side of the canyon . . . and how close they had come to being buried alongside Jacob Waltz's gold.

Jack came skidding to a halt in front of the pile of rocks. "What do I do now?" he called to them. "How am I supposed to put the gold back when there are all these ROCKS here?"

A jagged white line of lightning split the sky, and the air shook with thunder.

Boom! Boom!

When Henry looked up, the rim of the canyon was alight with a strange, almost phosphorescent glow.

"It's the Thunder God," Henry said, awed.

Fat drops of rain began to fall, splotching the dry ground.

"Is it trying to get us?" Jack cried, his eyes huge.

"Stop it," Simon ordered. "It's a storm, that's all. Help me move some of these rocks. The entrance to the mine has to be down below."

"There are too many rocks!" Jack wailed. "We'll never find it."

Gusts of wind blew through the canyon, whipping Delilah's braid across her face. She motioned to them. "It's this way, over here."

"How do you know?" Henry asked her.

"'Cuz when you guys went into the mine, I was standing out here waiting for a long time . . . and I remember the tunnel was under those drawings." She pointed at the high wall of the canyon, where Henry could see the petroglyph they'd discovered before—the crowd of tiny stick figures running and falling, a cascade of circles following them. Of course that's what the drawing was! A primitive picture of a rock slide. It was a warning from the ancient people who had lived here once . . . a warning about the Thunder God.

"Henry, help me roll this one," Simon directed, climbing over the pile of rocks.

Henry reached up and grabbed the rough side of a boulder, and he and Simon both strained to move it. Heaving, they managed to pry it loose.

"Watch out," Simon cried, as it tumbled to the canyon floor, barely missing Henry's foot.

The dark sky boiled overhead, and the rain was falling faster now, the drops as painful as pebbles hitting their skin. The wind picked up, and the temperature seemed to fall by several degrees in an instant.

Jack shoved the bag of gold in his pocket and crawled up the pile of rocks, pushing small boulders to the ground, which barely seemed to make a dent in the barricade. Delilah helped Simon and Henry tug on another large stone, but they were unable to budge it.

"This is *futile*," Henry cried in despair. "We will never be able to move all these rocks."

Simon shook his head grimly. "They're too heavy. Let's look for any kind of crack or hole that leads down toward the cave. Then you can drop the gold into it, Jack."

"But that's not the same as putting it back in the

mine," Jack shouted, over the building roar of the storm.

"It's the best we can do," Henry told him. "It will have to be enough."

Just then, the black sky opened overhead, and the rain poured down.

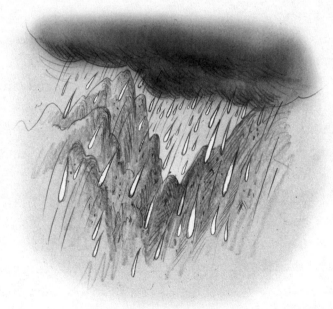

CHAPTER 24

REVENGE OF SUPERSTITION MOUNTAIN

"HERE!" DELILAH SHOUTED, pushing wet hair away from her face. "What about this?"

She was kneeling on the mountain of boulders, pointing to a triangular gap in the rocks. Rainwater coursed down it into the dark depths below.

"Good," Simon said. "Maybe the rain will wash the gold all the way down to the mine."

Jack, clutching his sandwich bag of flakes, looked forlorn. "What if it doesn't? What if that's not enough to break the curse?"

"It will be," Simon said, trying to take the plastic bag.

Henry stopped him. "He has to return the gold himself. Remember?"

"Yeah, you're right," Simon said. "Hurry, Jack. We need to get out of here. The storm is getting worse."

As if to confirm his words, another bolt of lightning sliced the dark sky, quickly followed by a deafening clap of thunder. Impossibly, the rain thickened, and the air shook with the mountain's disapproval.

It was the Thunder God—Henry knew it. He was angry and full of vengeance . . . but why now? What did the mountain want?

Was it Jack?

They were returning the gold. They were trying to make things right.

Jack looked at Henry in despair, rain plastering his hair to his head and streaming over his face. He opened the soaked plastic bag over the crevice in the rocks. "Do you think it will work?"

"Yes," Henry told him, with a certainty he didn't feel. "It will end the curse. It has to."

With trembling fingers, Jack opened the bag and overturned it above the gap in the rocks, shaking out the tiny flakes of gold. Even in the darkness of the storm, they glittered and sparkled. The rainwater had turned into a stream flowing down the canyon wall, and the golden specks floated on it like tiny enchanted boats,

swirling down, down, down, into the crack between the boulders.

"Get to the mine," Henry prayed under his breath. "Just find your way back to the Lost Dutchman's Mine."

"Is that all of it?" Simon asked, as Jack continued to shake the plastic bag.

He held it up to show them. It was empty.

Henry turned his face up to the sky, but if anything, it looked even blacker and more turbulent. The mountain's wrath was palpable.

"Let's go," Simon said, but just then Delilah grabbed his arm.

"Wait," she cried, her voice faint in the storm. "Look! What is that thing?"

Henry saw that she was pointing to a bundle of something wedged under a long ledge of rock. As he squinted through the heavy rain, he saw what appeared to be a cluster of thick cylinders wound together with a coiled wire. A small white-faced clock, as ordinary as a kitchen timer, was attached to the bundle. The whole contraption was lodged deep under the rock ledge, shielded from the driving rain.

"Oh, no. . . ." Simon recoiled. "It's dynamite!"

Dynamite! It looked like something from an old cartoon, Henry thought, like Bugs Bunny or Road Runner.

"The treasure hunters are here," Delilah gasped. "They're here right now."

Henry followed her gaze to the rim of the canyon. "Look! Up there!"

Through the heavy sheets of rain, he could just barely make out three blurred figures at the top of the rough slope, high above them.

"They must have set a timer," Simon shouted, his voice urgent. "We've got to get out of here." He scrambled backward down the mound of rocks.

"Is it going to explode?" Henry asked foolishly, suddenly numb.

"YES, Henry," Simon shouted. "Come on! Run!"

They began to crawl, slip, and tumble over the mountain of boulders, only to land in a muddy, rushing stream that was quickly covering the canyon floor.

"What's going on?" Jack yelled. "Why is there so much water?"

And then the roar of the storm drowned out their voices. Through the watery curtain of rain, Henry could only see vague, dark shapes.

He tried to claw his way along the wall of the canyon, tried to find Jack and Delilah, but his sneakers were full of water, and cold waves of it swirled around his legs, upsetting his balance.

The rain lashed his face, blinding him.

Faintly, as if at a great distance, he thought he heard Simon cry out.

"Flash flood!"

And then he was knocked off his feet and submerged.

CHAPTER 25
ALONE

THE WATER ROILED under and over Henry, sweeping him through the canyon. Rocks and branches scraped against his bare skin. His arms flailed wildly as he tried to grab on to something—anything—that would stop him. But the torrent was fast and furious.

Frantically, he tried to lift his feet and ride on the surface of the churning water. He remembered the time the Barker family had gone river rafting in Wyoming and the guide had said if you fell out of the raft, you should lift your feet and let yourself be carried by the water, so you wouldn't break a bone banging into the jagged rocks below.

"Simon!" he screamed, his voice instantly swallowed by the rushing creek and the storm. When he tried to turn his head to look for Jack and Delilah, the muddy water filled his nose and mouth.

Then something whacked his shoulder. He saw Delilah's wet face loom near him for an instant, her eyes huge with fright. For one brief second, his fingers grazed her arm.

"Delilah!" he yelled.

But the water swept her away.

Henry searched frantically for Jack, twisting in the torrent. Spitting and sputtering, he tried to breathe, as cold darkness closed over his head.

When Henry could open his eyes again, he found himself pressed against a huge, craggy rock. Looking around, he realized it was the head of the rock horse, rising out of the violent rapids. He spit and coughed wet mud from his mouth, wiping his face with his drenched T-shirt. The canyon was transformed by the impenetrable wall of rain and the rising creek that now roared through it. Turning toward the far end of the canyon, Henry could see that the water was rushing through a narrow slot, similar to the passageway they'd navigated to enter the canyon.

He didn't see Simon, Jack, or Delilah anywhere.

"Simon!" he cried. "Jack! Delilah!"

It seemed to him that he yelled their names again and again, craning into the storm and praying for a response.

But there was only the sound of the rain, and the frothy, swirling water below.

Henry blinked back tears. His throat ached. His shin had a long scrape on it, oozing blood, and his arms and knuckles were slashed and bruised. He stifled a sob.

Do the brave thing, he thought, *even if you don't feel brave.*

What would Uncle Hank do?

Find the others, of course. That's what he had to do. Still coughing, he climbed higher, toward the top of the rock horse. From the flat ledge of its head, he could see the whole canyon—the steep walls, the mound of boulders over the gold mine's entrance, and the swift, violent stream rushing over the canyon floor.

But there was no sign of his brothers or Delilah.

Carefully, Henry pulled off his wet T-shirt and wrung it out with both hands, trembling from the chill.

"Simon!" he yelled again, as loud as he could, waving his shirt back and forth through the air. Maybe Simon would see the pale arc of it through the storm. He waved it till his arm hurt, calling Simon's name over and over.

But the rain was so heavy, it was impossible to see anything.

Where were they? Henry slumped back down on the rock. What if they'd hit their heads? Or drowned? What if they were lost forever?

No.

Not like this. Suddenly, Henry was no longer afraid. A wave of pure rage filled him.

"NO!" he yelled. "STOP!"

He jumped to his feet and stamped on the flat rock, bellowing at the top of his lungs at the storm, the Thunder God, the mountain. The strange current of power and energy that had flooded him when he faced the mountain lion filled him again now. He screamed and jumped on the rock, waving his T-shirt through the air, not caring if he fell, not caring about anything at all.

And as suddenly as it had begun, the rain stopped.

Henry found himself standing alone on the drenched rock, perched over the canyon and the roaring creek. He looked around in wonder. He was shaking from cold, and his voice was hoarse.

Was the mountain listening?

And then he heard it . . . a thin sound that carried faintly above the roar of the churning water.

"Henry! Henry! Over here!"

CHAPTER 26
MISSING

It was Simon.

He was climbing over the rocks along the side of the canyon, a few feet above the water, waving at Henry and yelling.

"Simon!" Henry cried, scrambling down off the head of the rock horse. "I'm coming!"

He crawled and clambered over to the side of the canyon, slipping on the wet boulders. Simon was climbing awkwardly toward him. His face and clothing were streaked with mud, and there were small bloody scrapes all over his arms.

"Are you okay?" Simon asked. "I heard you yelling and I kept shouting at you, but you couldn't hear me."

"Yeah, I'm fine," Henry said. He shivered, pulling

his wet T-shirt back over his head. "But we have to find Jack and Delilah."

"I know. I don't see them anywhere." Simon's face was grim. "And I lost the backpack. It just disappeared."

"What do you think happened? Where did all the water come from?"

"It was a flash flood," Simon said. "It happens when there's a heavy rain in a dry place like this. Remember? Emmett told us about them a long time ago. There must be a creek at the other end of the canyon. When it started raining so hard, it flooded."

"It's so much water," Henry said in amazement, watching the brown stream that frothed and splashed through the canyon, disappearing into the narrow slot at the canyon's entrance.

"Hen, we have to find Jack and Delilah and get out of here," Simon said. "If that dynamite explodes, the rocks will fly everywhere."

Henry turned his worried gaze onto the steep pile of boulders hiding the entrance to the mine. "Do you think it's still there, after the rain and the flood?"

"I don't know, but it was tucked under that ledge. And we can't wait around to find out."

Henry looked up to the rim of the canyon, where he

had seen the blurred figures huddled right before the flood. It was utterly still now. There was no sign of anyone.

Overhead, the dark sky seemed to be turning a shade lighter, with a strange brightness struggling to break through.

"Jack! Delilah!" They both began yelling, their voices overlapping, as they climbed along the canyon wall. They scanned the creek and the rocks for any sign of movement.

"Jack!"

"Delilah! Where are you?"

Henry had no idea how much time had passed. It seemed like hours since the flood, but he knew that couldn't be right. The darkness of the storm had been disorienting. What if the mountain had taken them? He thought of Sara Delgado, lost in the canyons, coming back so changed and strange. He tried to shake off the chill of fear. That couldn't happen to Delilah and Jack. It just couldn't.

"Wait—over there!" Simon pointed toward the narrow chute that led to the first canyon. Henry saw a flash of pink—Delilah's pink backpack, stained with water and mud, swinging over the rocks. Delilah was with it.

"Hey!" she yelled.

Henry's heart leapt in his chest. She was all right! She had survived!

"I found it! I found it!"

She was clambering excitedly toward them, her wet face flushed with exertion.

"What?" Simon asked. "Your backpack?"

But Henry understood. She was waving something small and silver in her hand. It was her father's compass.

"Where did you find it?" he asked in wonderment.

"Your compass?" Simon looked incredulous. "But you didn't even lose it here. You dropped it in the other canyon."

"I know," Delilah exclaimed. "I never thought to look for it here. It was in the rocks. I don't even know how I saw it. But I did! I found it! I found it!"

She had reached them now, her soaked braid dangling over her shoulder, her face suffused with joy.

Simon was shaking his head, stupefied. "I guess an animal or bird could have carried it here. Birds like shiny things."

"It's not even wet," Delilah continued, exultant. "It's a little scratched, but it works fine." She threw her arms around both of them, hugging them tight. "I'm so glad we're all okay!"

Then she stopped. "Where's Jack?"

Henry could feel the weight of his worry pinning him to the rock. "We don't know. We can't find him."

Simon's face was tense. "We've been looking everywhere," he said, staring into the turbulent water still streaming through the canyon.

"Jack is strong," Delilah said quickly. "I'm sure he's okay."

"What about the curse?" Henry said slowly.

"There is no curse, Henry," Simon snapped. "Stop saying that."

"Then where is he? What if he's lost like Sara Delgado? What if we find him and he's not the same?"

"Let's just find him first," Simon said, still peering into the muddy torrent. "And quickly."

Delilah tightened her thin arm around Henry's shoulders. "We returned the gold to the mine," she said. "The mountain isn't angry at us anymore. I can feel it, Henry—I got my dad's compass back."

She lifted it in her palm, looking at the shining glass face. The needle trembled and swung to the black *N*, pointing north.

Henry's gaze followed the arrow to a promontory of rock that jutted out next to Delilah, curving around her.

He could see an array of faint white drawings covering it, sheltered from the rest of the canyon.

"More petroglyphs," he said absently, tapping his finger against the rock.

But Simon was already elbowing past him, scrutinizing the small white figures.

"Hey, you guys," he said. "Look at this. It's a picture of a flood."

Henry saw that he was right. The drawing showed tiny stick figures fleeing from a curled wave of water that

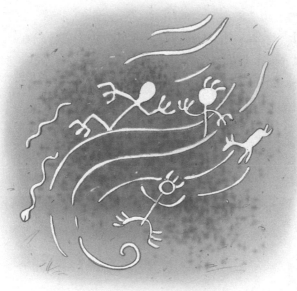

seemed to be chasing them. Some were falling underneath it. Others were floating on its surface.

"Look at these guys," Delilah said. "They climbed out of the way."

She pointed to a handful of figures that seemed to be standing and sitting in a cave, above the silhouette of a horse.

"That's the rock horse," Simon said. "There must be a cave over here, in the wall of the canyon."

They scrambled backward over the boulders, so they could survey the steep contours of the canyon wall.

"Do you see anything?" Simon asked.

Delilah shook her head. "Not a cave, anyway."

But then Henry *did* see something. A dark hollow, and a patch of blue.

"That's Jack's shirt," he cried.

CHAPTER 27
ESCAPE FROM SUPERSTITION MOUNTAIN

FRANTICALLY, THEY ALL BEGAN CLIMBING toward the small splotch of blue poking out of the rocks.

"Jack!" Simon yelled.

"Jack!" Henry echoed, with Delilah calling behind him, "Jack, are you okay?"

There was no response from the small cavern. The patch of blue didn't move.

"Hurry," Simon urged them, climbing recklessly over the rocks.

"It's got to be Jack," Delilah said. "The mountain was pointing us to him."

Simon got there first, grabbing the sharp ledge of rock and hauling himself over it, with Henry and Delilah tumbling quickly after him.

"Jack!" Simon cried.

Henry's heart seized. Jack was lying on his stomach in a dark, spreading puddle of water, his hair plastered to his scalp, his eyes closed. His clothing was drenched, and Henry could see that his arms and legs were covered with the same scrapes and bruises that the others had suffered. He wasn't moving.

Simon crouched next to him, gripping his shoulder and shaking it. Moments later, Delilah and Henry knelt beside him.

"We have to make sure he's breathing," Simon said, quickly leaning over Jack's face. "Roll him on his back."

"Jack . . . Jack . . ." Henry cried, helping Simon turn him over. He had a brief terrible thought of the curse, but he instantly banished it from his mind. They had returned the gold. The storm had stopped. The mountain had given back Delilah's compass, and she was right; the petroglyphs had led them here. The mountain was speaking to them now.

Simon pressed his head against Jack's soaked T-shirt. "I can hear his heart beating," he said, "I can hear him breathing."

Henry nearly collapsed with relief. "Why isn't he waking up?"

"I'll clear his mouth," Simon said. "Maybe he's not getting enough air."

Simon turned Jack's head to the side and swept his finger between Jack's lips, dislodging a wad of mud.

"His mouth is full of stuff." For a second, Simon raised his eyes to Henry's, and Henry saw only naked fear. To see it on Simon's face—Simon, the one who always knew what to do—shocked him.

"It's okay," he told Simon. "He's going to be fine."

Simon scooped with two fingers this time, and suddenly Jack's eyes opened and he lurched up from the ground, coughing and choking, gasping for breath.

Simon hit him on the back, and muddy water spewed out of his nose and mouth, while Jack continued to suck in great rasping lungfuls of air.

"It's okay, it's okay," Delilah said, patting his back. "You'll be all right now."

Jack continued to cough and sneeze. The panicked look slowly receded from his pale face.

Simon dropped to the floor of the cave, covering his face in his hands. His shoulders were shaking.

Henry realized with a start that he was crying.

Delilah quickly knelt beside him. "Jack's all right, Simon. Look, he's breathing now. He's sitting up."

Simon's breath came in sobs. "He almost drowned."

"But he didn't," Henry said firmly.

"Yeah, I didn't drown," Jack said, looking worriedly at Simon. "I'm okay now."

Henry had a sudden, crystal-clear understanding of what it must feel like to be the oldest . . . the responsible one, the one who had to know what to do. Simon made the decisions. He knew how dangerous things actually were. If something had happened to Jack, Simon would have believed forevermore that it was his fault.

But already Simon was settling back into himself, taking deep breaths, squaring his shoulders. "How did you get way up here?" he asked Jack.

Jack wiped his mouth on his mud-streaked shirt. "I don't know! I went underwater. That's the last thing I remember. I thought it was the curse," he whispered, his lips trembling.

"No," Henry told him, now certain. "The mountain saved you. We found some more petroglyphs—pictures of people in a flood—and they showed us where you were."

When Jack looked at him blankly, Delilah explained, "The pictures were of people in this little cave, above the rock horse. That's how we knew where to find you."

"You must have climbed up here," Simon told him.

Jack shook his head. "I don't remember that."

Simon stood up, gazing over the canyon, his eyes narrow. "Well, are you okay to keep climbing? Because if that dynamite explodes, we may never get out of here."

Jack nodded, wobbling to his feet. "Are the bad guys still up there?"

"I don't see them now," Delilah said, squinting across the canyon at the opposite rim. "But they were there, right before the flood."

Simon was still looking at the canyon floor, where the water frothed and churned. "We can't go back through the pass to the other canyon. There's too much water."

Henry saw that he was right. The roiling stream had charged into the narrow chute, filling it. "We'll have to climb up this side," he said. "And try to find our way back."

Simon nodded, rubbing his hand through his damp hair. "I wish I still had my backpack . . . and the rope and shovel."

Delilah grinned. "We'll be fine," she said. "We have my dad's compass." Securing her pink backpack over her shoulders, she hoisted herself onto the rocky overhang that shielded the cave.

The boys followed her, gripping first with their hands, then wedging their feet into the rock for a purchase. With Delilah leading the way, they began their ascent up the wall of the canyon.

By the time they reached the rim, the cloud cover had lifted, and the sky was filled with a sharp, uncertain light. Henry's T-shirt was starting to dry, but his sneakers squelched at every step. When he glanced at the others, he thought what a miserable picture they made—wet, muddy, and bedraggled, sporting various bloody scrapes and scratches. What would they tell their mother? Even if they washed themselves off, they would still look like some awful mishap had befallen them.

"What time is it?" he asked Simon.

"Late afternoon, I think," Simon said. "My watch got wet, and now it's not working."

"It's three-thirty," Delilah announced, brandishing the bright pink sports watch on her wrist. At Simon's double take, she shrugged. "Waterproof."

Pink and *waterproof* didn't seem like they should go together, in Henry's opinion, but it somehow didn't surprise him that Delilah had a waterproof watch.

"That means we only have an hour and a half before

Mom and Dad get home," Simon said. "And we need time to clean up. Hurry!"

Henry wondered how it could be possible that they'd climbed up the mountain, scared off a mountain lion, climbed down into the canyon, returned Jack's gold to the mine, discovered dynamite, and survived a flash flood, and they still had an hour and a half left before their parents returned from their outing. It might not be enough time to get home and washed up, but it seemed pretty good, considering.

He pictured his parents with Aunt Kathy and Emmett in the midst of their civilized Sunday afternoon, wandering through the vast, quiet galleries of the Phoenix Art Museum, while the boys and Delilah were here on Superstition Mountain fighting for their very lives. One day he wanted to tell them all about these adventures. Not now . . . it was too soon, and because they were parents, if they heard anything about it now, they would feel required to *do* something. But one day. Looking around at the red-brown landscape of cliffs and canyons and rocky spires, Henry made a promise to himself that he would remember every detail.

They crawled over rocks into the scraggly woods that bordered the canyon.

"We need to head south," Simon said. "That should be the way home."

"Okay," Delilah said, holding the compass outstretched in her palm and assessing it. "This way."

They were just starting into the woods, picking their way along the lip of the canyon, when the mountain's stillness was shattered by a sudden, shocking *BOOM!*

BOOM-BOOM-BOOM-BOOM!

The noise was deafening. Henry could barely understand what was happening. When the ground shook and Delilah started to topple backward, he instinctively grabbed the strap of her backpack and held on. They both dropped to the ground, wrapping their arms over their heads.

BOOM! BOOM! BOOM!

"It's the dynamite!" Simon yelled, and Henry pressed his arms tighter against his ears.

The noise ceased, and when he raised his head, Henry saw that the mounds of rocks that had covered the entrance to the Lost Dutchman's Mine were now blasted to smithereens, leaving a gaping hole in the side of the canyon. "Look! The mine!" he cried, but as they all stared in shock, they heard another noise . . . a familiar building rumble. To Henry's horror, he saw that the top of the canyon wall appeared to be breaking loose, and rock after rock fell through air.

"Avalanche!" Simon yelled. "Run!"

They all leapt to their feet and raced over the shifting, shaking ground, running as fast and as far from the canyon as their legs would take them. As he scrambled and jumped through the brush, Henry paused, just once, to glance over his shoulder. He saw the sides of the canyon tumbling down. Rocks broke away and fell, barreling

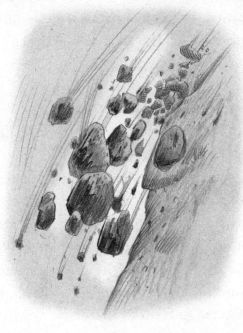

through space, filling the hole in the canyon wall where the mine had been, and then filling the canyon itself—until, Henry realized, there wasn't even a canyon anymore.

Had the treasure hunters really believed they could outsmart Superstition Mountain? That a little dynamite would make the gold theirs? It seemed ridiculous to Henry now. Of course the mountain would keep what belonged to it—at whatever cost.

Frantically, the boys and Delilah stumbled through the trees and brush, tripping and sliding in the pebbly dirt. *Home*, Henry thought. *We have to get home.*

CHAPTER 28
SANCTUARY

"Wow, THAT WAS COOL!" Jack exclaimed, as they clambered through dense brush, searching for any hint of a trail, aware of the sudden silence. "Did you see all those rocks falling?"

"Yeah," Simon said. "The explosion caused another avalanche, a much bigger one than before."

"Or it was the mountain," Henry said softly. "The gold will stay there forever."

"I wonder if Julia Thomas and the others were in the canyon when the dynamite exploded," Delilah said.

"I didn't see anyone on the rim," Simon said. "And if they were watching, they couldn't have stayed there for long. The entire wall came down."

"Do you think they were caught in the avalanche?" Henry asked, suddenly worried. As awful as the treasure hunters were, and as many times as they had tried to cause trouble for the boys and Delilah, he couldn't bear to think of them being crushed by a mountain of falling rock. He remembered how terrified he had felt during the first avalanche, when the stream of loose boulders had buried the gold mine.

"I hope so," Jack declared, unfazed. "They are the bad guys."

"They're"—Henry hesitated, searching for the right word—"*unscrupulous*," he said finally. "But I don't think they deserve to die."

"I didn't see them anywhere when we were climbing out," Simon said. "And they put the dynamite there, so I'm pretty sure they knew not to hang around. I'm just glad it didn't explode sooner. We'd have been trapped . . . or worse."

Henry shuddered, just thinking about it.

Delilah, who had been forging a trail with her father's compass, came to a halt. "We're still going south," she said, peering through the brush. "But it looks like there are two paths here. Which one should we take?"

They had come to the junction of two ragged trails, which didn't even look like trails to Henry . . . more like the haphazard, matted hoof paths left by deer.

Simon squinted in both directions. "I don't know. And we don't have much time."

They stood in the mountain's stillness, listening to the twittering of birds and faint rustlings in the brush. Which way?

"We'll just have to choose," Simon said. "What do you think, Hen?"

Henry turned to him in surprise. Was Simon really asking him what to do? He felt both the weight of the responsibility and the thrill of something else, some sense of taking charge, being the one the others could rely on. Maybe this, too, was what it felt like to be Simon.

"This way," Henry decided. And he strode down the path, the others trotting behind him.

After a while of breaking through brush and shimmying over rocks, they rounded a bend, and Henry saw something up ahead.

Something small.

Something black.

Something that darted through the gray-green shrubs and boulders, barely pausing to cast an appraising glance in their direction.

"Look! It's Josie!" Henry cried.

Simon's face broke into a grin. "Then you chose the right way, Hen! She must be heading home."

And so they followed Josie's sure and graceful course down the mountain, until at last the brush cleared and the ground became more level. Behind the statuary of cactuses, with their raised, welcoming arms, the rooftops of the houses of Superstition gleamed in the late-afternoon light. There was the roof of Uncle Hank's house, their home on the edge of the desert. It shone like a beacon, guiding them out of the foothills. Finally, they were home.

It was nearly five o'clock when they burst through the sliding glass door into the kitchen. The house was an oasis of cool and calm, the only noise the low hum of the air conditioner. Oddly, the deck and the yard were bone dry. The violent storm on the mountain had clearly bypassed Superstition. As they hurried into the hallway, the phone rang, jangling urgently in the quiet.

Simon grabbed it, and Henry saw him stiffen. "Oh, hey . . . hey, Mom." He pressed his finger to his lips and widened his eyes at the others. "Oh, you have? For the last two hours? Sorry! Yeah, yeah, we're all here. We're fine. We were just outside, in the desert . . . practicing rock climbing on some big boulders." He hesitated, shrugging at Henry. "Um, we got a little scraped up—you know, from jumping and climbing."

He held the phone away from his ear so that they could all hear Mrs. Barker reacting to that. Her voice raised an octave, sounding thin and worried through the phone. But it was good, Henry thought, to prepare their parents now for the mess of cuts and bruises they would see when they got home.

Henry heard his mother say, "What? What do you mean, scraped up? Are you hurt? Did Jack fall?"

"No, we're fine. Our clothes are dirty. I'll put them in the washing machine," Simon told her soothingly. "Yeah, we're all here—Delilah too. She's going home right now." He covered the receiver with his hand and whispered to Delilah, "You'd better go. Our mom called your house and got your mom all worked up wondering where you were."

Delilah nodded, lifting her backpack from the floor. "See you tomorrow," she whispered. She smiled at Henry, and he saw that she was holding her father's compass tightly in her hand.

"I'm glad you found your compass," he said. "Even if you didn't need to."

Her look was suddenly shy. "Me too! It makes me feel

different about the mountain," she said softly. "Know what I mean?"

Henry nodded. "I feel different about the mountain too."

With her brown braid bouncing against her back, Delilah turned and ran through the hallway to the front door. A minute later, Henry saw her hunched over the handlebars of her bike, speeding down the Barkers' driveway.

Simon was still on the phone but silent, as Henry heard their mother's voice prattling with tinny insistence through the earpiece. "I'm really sorry! We lost track of time," Simon said, rolling his eyes now. "Mom, this is why I need a cell phone. I know you said I had to wait till eighth grade, but I really think I should have one now."

Henry could never get over how easily Simon turned their parents' frustration with him to his own advantage.

"Well, okay, but I'm just saying," Simon continued. "You could have talked to us whenever you wanted this afternoon if I'd had a cell phone. Okay, here's Hen."

Henry took the phone with trepidation. "Hello?"

"Henry!" his mother exclaimed. "Sweetie, where have you been all afternoon? We called and called—I even called Delilah's mother!"

"Sorry, Mom," he said. For some reason, hearing his mother's voice made him want to cry . . . even more than the storm and the flood and losing Jack had made him want to cry. It was as if all the emotions from their experience on the mountain were suddenly welling up in him, about to spill over, because his mom was here on the phone, worried about him, and now he finally *could* cry. He didn't have to keep being brave. He gulped and tried to calm himself.

"We're all okay. Sorry we weren't home when you called."

"Henry, what's the matter?" his mother asked instantly. "What happened?"

Simon shook his head ferociously, reaching for the phone, but Henry sucked in a deep breath and said determinedly, "Nothing. We finished the garage! It looks . . . *meticulous.*"

Mrs. Barker laughed. "Well, great, that's a big help. And we have some news for you three, but we'll wait and tell you in person."

"Good news or bad news?" Henry asked.

"Oh, good! Very good! We're running late, but we'll be home in an hour and you'll hear it all then. Now put Jack on."

He handed the phone to Jack, and as he and Simon drifted back toward the bedroom, shedding clothes as they went, they could hear him whining to be told the news.

When their parents walked through the door with Aunt Kathy and Emmett an hour later, the boys were freshly washed and clean—after what seemed like the longest shower Henry had taken in his entire life. The water running down the drain was pure brown at first, and it took endless iterations of soap and shampoo to finally turn it clear. They had put Neosporin on the worst of their cuts, and Jack was sporting three Band-Aids, at his insistence. Simon had dumped all of their clothes in the wash, along with their pajamas and a few towels, and the washing machine was merrily chugging away, erasing the last remnants of the dusty climb and the flash flood.

"We're here!" Aunt Kathy sang out, bustling into the kitchen. She dumped her large handbag on the counter and scooped Henry into her arms, burying her face in his wet curls. "You smell so good!" she exclaimed. "But oh my heavens, Henry, what did you do to yourself? And Jack! So many Band-Aids! You look like you were run over by a lawn mower!"

Mrs. Barker's face seized in horror at the sight of them. "What on earth were you boys doing?" she cried, dropping to her knees on the kitchen floor to examine Henry's shin. "You're so banged up!"

"We were just fooling around, Mom," Simon said, attempting nonchalance. "I told you, we were rock climbing, and we got . . . carried away."

Yeah, swept away, Henry was thinking. *By a flash flood!*

"Did you fall? Was anyone hurt?" Mrs. Barker had moved over to Jack now, but the generous application of Band-Aids made it more difficult for her to assess his wounds. "It looks like you were in a fight!"

"Yeah," Mr. Barker agreed. "If this is what you look like, I want to see the rocks."

"You must have been over by the quarry," Emmett said. "You need to be careful out there. That ravine is deep."

Quarry? Henry and Simon exchanged glances, and Henry knew exactly what Simon was thinking. How could they have gone all summer without knowing about the quarry?

"Tell us the NEWS! Tell us the NEWS!" Jack chanted impatiently. "You promised as soon as you got home!"

Aunt Kathy clapped her hands, flushed and beaming. "Okay, okay! Anybody want to guess?" Henry saw that she was wiggling her fingers in excitement . . . and then he saw the reason for her excitement. On the third finger of her left hand was a small, round, sparkling diamond.

"You're getting married!" he cried. "To Emmett?"

Aunt Kathy threw back her head and laughed her jolly, rolling laugh. "Of *course* to Emmett, silly! Who else would I be marrying?"

"But it's so soon," Simon said.

"Well . . ." Aunt Kathy smiled. "Sometimes you just know."

"Does that mean . . ." Henry looked from one to the other. "Are you moving here, to Arizona?"

"Not right away—I need to find a job first—but soon! And then I'll get to see you boys all the time!"

"YAY!" Jack screamed, tackling her around the waist. "That'll be GREAT!"

Henry's smile was so wide he thought it would split his face in half. Aunt Kathy and Emmett!

"Do we have to call you Uncle Emmett?" Simon asked thoughtfully. "Because we're kind of used to just calling you Emmett."

"You can call me whatever you want," Emmett said, grinning. He tucked his arm around Aunt Kathy's waist and pulled her close.

And in the joyful celebration that followed, the many unanswered questions about the boys' lost afternoon and battered condition were forgotten, at least temporarily.

CHAPTER 29
NAMESAKE

A WEEK LATER, on a blazing hot Arizona day, Henry, Simon, Jack, and Delilah found themselves standing in front of the Barker tombstone in the cemetery, in the surprising presence of Aunt Kathy, Emmett, and their parents . . . and the shocking company of Prita Alchesay.

What a week it had been! First, the whole town had been turned upside down by the disappearance of three well-known citizens—the librarian Julia Thomas, Officer Myers, and the cemetery caretaker Richard Delgado. Richard Delgado's brown sedan had been found in a cul-de-sac near a trail leading to Superstition Mountain, and a neighbor reported seeing three people set off toward the mountain on Sunday morning. A search party was hastily organized, and for two days, policemen and a volunteer search-and-rescue crew fanned out over the mountain, looking for the three treasure hunters. To Jack's immense satisfaction, a helicopter had even been called in.

The boys and Delilah were greatly relieved not to have to confess to seeing the treasure hunters on the mountain. But as the search continued, they grew more and more worried that the three had been injured or killed in the explosion and avalanche—that was, until various suspicious items came to light during the police investigation. There was evidence of dynamite at Officer Myers's home and of hasty packing at Julia Thomas's apartment. Most important, the police discovered that Sara Delgado was also missing, along with some of the contents of the Delgado home. And so the search was called off, and a full-scale investigation began into the suspected illegal activities of three of Superstition's most prominent citizens.

After endless discussion—in which Simon carefully weighed pros and cons, Henry wavered in moral uncertainty, and Jack grew ever more anxious to take action, regardless of the consequences—the boys had finally decided to share with their parents one of their biggest discoveries from their forays into Uncle Hank's desk: the existence of Prita. It was the only way they could think of to get permission to return to the cemetery and dig up the Barker gravesite.

"What?" Mrs. Barker had exclaimed when they told her about Prita. "He had a girlfriend? A longtime girlfriend? This is the first I've heard of such a thing, and I have to tell you, that does not jibe with his . . . reputation."

"Not just a girlfriend," Henry had corrected her. "A great love."

"Why, that old dawg," Mr. Barker had said, chuckling. "Keeping it hidden from all of us. But I can believe it. Uncle Hank was a person of big tastes. Big adventures, big loves."

"Well, I would certainly like to meet her," their mother continued. "We'll have her over for dinner sometime."

"This will be great," Mr. Barker crowed, rubbing his hands together just like Simon often did. "With Kathy moving down here and marrying Emmett, and now this Prita lady, we are going to have more family in Arizona than we had back in Illinois."

Henry smiled, because he realized that, amazingly, although he'd lost his old uncle Hank, he would be gaining a new uncle, Emmett. And he started thinking that, unlike Simon, he might actually want to call him Uncle Emmett.

Mr. Barker continued enthusiastically, "I can't wait to see who turns up next! Maybe ol' Uncle Hank had a kid or two we never knew about."

Mrs. Barker shot him a disapproving glance. "Jim," she said sternly. "And anyway, if he did, they would be older than you."

"I know! Wouldn't that be interesting?"

"Actually," Simon interrupted, "we wanted you to meet Prita soon. Like, maybe tomorrow."

"Tomorrow?" Mrs. Barker raised her eyebrows. "What's happening tomorrow?"

And that was how they delicately broached the subject of their visit to Prita, and the note Uncle Hank left for Henry, and their discovery that the Barker monument in the cemetery was a grave plot belonging to Uncle Hank, where something might be buried that he intended for the boys to have.

"Whoa, whoa, whoa," Mr. Barker said. "We can't just go digging up graves without some sort of permission from the cemetery. And that is going to be difficult to come by, since Richard Delgado has skipped town."

Simon and Henry exchanged glances.

"We can show you the records at the cemetery," Simon said. "You'll see that he owns that plot—doesn't that mean we inherit it, along with the rest of his stuff? And come on, Dad, why would he put the name Barker on the tombstone? It doesn't make sense. It's our name, not his, and anyway, he was cremated."

"I admit that's funny," Mr. Barker said. "But what in the world do you think he could have left buried at the cemetery? There wasn't anything mentioned in his will."

"But he left me that note, Dad," Henry said. "There's something he wants us to find."

And then Mr. Barker had held up his hands in capitulation, and he had gamely spent the last day or two at the lawyer's office and the police station, finally gaining the needed permission to open the grave site, where, as it turned out, there was no record of human burial.

Now, over Mrs. Barker's protests, here they all were, at the grave site with the Barker tombstone, with Aunt Kathy, Emmett, and Prita herself, who was standing shyly to one side near Mrs. Barker, who kept gently engaging her in conversation.

"Start digging!" Jack yelled, jumping up and down.

"Settle down, Jack," Mrs. Barker reproved him, glancing at Prita. "I still don't think you should get your hopes up."

"You boys had better appreciate how much trouble I went to, getting permission to do this," Mr. Barker complained. "I had to talk to about six different people."

"We do, Dad!" they chorused.

So Emmett and Mr. Barker started digging, driving their shovels into the hard earth, overturning it next to the grave site. Henry crouched on the ground, his chin in his hands, watching. He had brought Uncle Hank's note with him to the cemetery and now sat with it clutched inside his fist like a good-luck charm. Would there be anything down there? He thought of the book *Treasure Island*, with its pirates digging for treasure, and *The Adventures of Huckleberry Finn*, with Huck hiding money in a coffin to keep it safe. *What did you leave behind for me, Uncle Hank?* Henry wondered. *Besides your name.*

Meanwhile, Mrs. Barker and Aunt Kathy chatted with Prita, coaxing her with questions, to which she seemed to respond hesitantly, but with tolerant amusement.

"I just think it's so romantic," Aunt Kathy was

saying. "You wrote love letters to each other! Nobody does that anymore. Nobody even knows cursive anymore. We have texts and e-mails, but nothing that somebody bothered to write longhand on paper. And he saved your letters, all this time."

Prita just smiled, nodding.

"We're very happy to have found you," Mrs. Barker added. "And I do hope you'll come over and join us for dinner. I'd love to get to know you better, especially because you were so important to Uncle Hank."

"I'd like that," Prita said. "I want to know all of you better too. He talked about you so often, and I see him in your husband." She paused. "And the boys." Her eyes rested on Henry, and he looked back at her, smiling.

Henry suddenly realized that the end point of life wasn't a cemetery. How could it be? Life went on and on, in letters and desks and inherited houses, in loves that lasted, in the tiny mysterious particles of genetic material that flowed through Uncle Hank and Mr. Barker and now through Henry himself. Uncle Hank wasn't gone. He was still here, in all of them, in so many different ways.

"Hey!" Mr. Barker said. "I hit something."

He and Emmett began to dig more earnestly now, heaving large shovelfuls of dirt to the side. Delilah came to sit beside Henry, crossing her legs. Her eyes were bright with excitement. "Do you think it's there?" she whispered. "The deathbed ore of Jacob Waltz?"

Henry looked at her, his heart full. It was hard to explain, but he wasn't sure it mattered to him if the gold was there. Uncle Hank had given him so much already. He sighed. The first week of school loomed ahead, and their summer of marvelous adventures was shrinking to an end. But here was Delilah, his friend Delilah, and they would be in the same grade together this year.

"Huh," Emmett said. "It's a box of some sort."

A candle box? Henry wondered.

"Here, give me a hand," Mr. Barker said.

Together, they stooped and lifted the box out of the hole, setting it on the grass. It was a wooden container, splintered and crusted with dirt. When Emmett brushed it off, Henry could see remnants of faded paint. He scrambled onto his knees, leaning forward to get a better look.

"Is this what you boys were expecting?" Mr. Barker asked him. "What do you think is inside?"

Prita quietly moved away from Mrs. Barker and Aunt Kathy and came over to the edge of the hole. "Open it," she said softly.

Mr. Barker glanced at her, intrigued. "Ready?"

Slowly he lifted the lid.

Henry almost fell into the hole. Delilah gasped. Simon knotted his hands together in amazement, and Jack let out a whoop that could have been heard all the way in the center of town.

There in the box was a mound of GOLD, shining, flashing, sparkling gold—more gold nuggets than Henry had seen in his entire life. They were as individual as pebbles or snowflakes or pieces of popcorn—piled on top of each other, flashing brilliantly in the sunshine.

Prita's calm, lined face broke into a slow smile. "So Hank *did* find it," she said, satisfied. "The deathbed ore of Jacob Waltz."

Emmett laughed in astonishment. "You mean it's true? I thought that was just a legend!"

Mr. Barker was crouched next to the candle box, sifting the nuggets through his fingers. "Unbelievable," he said, shaking his head. "Is it real?"

"It certainly seems real. . . . Look how it shines," Aunt Kathy gasped.

"What in the world is all this?" Mrs. Barker cried. "Who does it belong to?"

"To you," Prita said. "To all of you, but especially to the boys. He left this for them."

"But what about you?" Delilah asked. "Didn't he leave anything for you?"

Prita smiled at her. "Oh yes, my dear. Much more than you know. The gold is not for me. It was the one thing that came between us, and look how he protected me, by not telling me he found it. The gold is for the boys."

And Henry, who had been speechless through the whole discovery, now sat back on his heels and opened his fist, spreading Uncle Hank's note on the grass next to his knees.

Delilah leaned close to him, reading it with him, her shoulder almost but not quite touching his.

Dear Henry,

Your name is my name. It will outlast death—the way a place can be about death but outlast death. If you believe that, you'll know where to find something I left for you and your brothers. Live well, Henry.

Love, Uncle Hank

My name is his name, Henry thought. I'm his name-sake. And he understood suddenly that *legacy* was a word that pointed in two directions, backward to the past and forward to the future. And the connection between the past and the future was Henry himself.

He raised his eyes to the shadow-filled cliffs of Super-stition Mountain, rising behind the cemetery. He thought of all they had found there, not just the canyon and the skulls, the saddlebag and coins and map, and even the

Lost Dutchman's Mine and the gold—but what he'd found in himself, buried deep inside where he had not known it existed . . . a thirst for adventure, a steely thread of courage, and a willingness to take risks for something or someone that mattered more than himself. The mountain, which had seemed so terrifying, had shown him the best parts of himself.

He read the last lines of the note one more time.

Live well, Henry.

And there, under the scorching sun, in the middle of the desert, in the shadow of the vast, strange, unforgettable mountain, Uncle Hank's words shimmered and shifted in Henry's mind, morphing from a wish to a command to a promise.

I will, Henry thought.

I will.

AUTHOR'S NOTE

It is strange to be writing the final author's note for the Superstition Mountain trilogy. There is still so much to say about this fantastical place.

While Superstition is an imaginary town and the trilogy's cast of contemporary characters is entirely fictitious, all the historic figures mentioned are real or based on fact. The details of the mountain landscape are very true, and the Thunder God described in the book is a genuine part of the Apache belief system. According to the Apache, the Thunder God is the deity that protects the Superstition Mountain range and its gold; they believe that he resents intruders in the mountains and that he is the force responsible for the terrible fates that have befallen people searching for the gold.

Ken-tee, the young Apache woman who purportedly led Jacob Waltz to the mountain's gold in the late 1800s, is a prominent figure in the region's folklore. It is unclear whether she ever existed. According to legend, when her tribe discovered that she had revealed the location of the gold to Waltz, they cut out her tongue to punish her for her betrayal.

The description of the "deathbed ore of Jacob Waltz" is similarly shrouded in legend. The most common version of the tale is this: as Jacob Waltz lay dying from pneumonia he had contracted during a flood, he told Julia Thomas, the neighbor who was caring for him, about a candle box of gold ore that he kept under his bed. On the day that he died, after she left his bedside to get a doctor, two men came into the house and stole the so-called deathbed ore from its hiding place under the bed. For many years, this famed candle box of gold was the object of much speculation and pursuit.

The Superstition Mountain range remains a dangerous place where visitors should travel with care. The Pinal and Maricopa County sheriff's offices send search-and-rescue crews into the mountains approximately thirty times a year to look for missing persons. Since 2009, there have been at least seven deaths and one unsolved disappearance in the Superstitions. Most often, the victims are ill-prepared hikers or treasure hunters searching for the Lost Dutchman's Mine.

If you decide to visit this strange and mesmerizing place, please be careful! Make sure you go with an adult; plan your hike thoroughly; take plenty of water and sunscreen; and *stay on the trail*. It is well worth the trip. Rich in history and folklore, the Superstitions are full of the magical lure of the frontier: a place where different peoples clash and mix; where human endurance in the harshest of environments is repeatedly tested; and where untold riches await. After writing this trilogy, I feel like Henry did on his final trip up the mountain: Superstition Mountain has become a part of me.

ACKNOWLEDGMENTS

A SERIES IS A MUCH BIGGER, more complicated project than a single novel, and my indebtedness has grown proportionately. I am profoundly grateful to the following people for their help in the creation of this final book in the Superstition Mountain trilogy:

My wonderful editor and friend, Christy Ottaviano, whose curiosity and warm encouragement have nurtured many literary leaps—in this case leading me to write a series, something I doubt I would have been brave enough to undertake otherwise.

My excellent agent, Edward Necarsulmer IV, who is always in my corner, and who helps me balance the business of writing with the art of it.

The hardworking editorial, design, marketing, and sales departments at Holt, who have done such a terrific job of introducing my books to readers.

My circle of writer friends—lovely companions in an otherwise solitary profession: Nora Baskin, Jane Burns, Jane Kamensky, Jill Lepore, Bennett Madison, Natalie Standiford, Chris Tebbetts, and Ellen Wittlinger.

My incredible readers, who have made my books so much better with their insights, questions, and suggestions: Mary Broach, Jane Burns, Claire Carlson, Laura Forte, Jane Kamensky, Carol Sheriff, and Zoe Wheeler. Special thanks to my younger readers, Anna Daileader Sheriff and Ben Daileader Sheriff, for their helpful comments on the first draft of this book.

And finally and most of all, I am indebted to my family—Ward, Zoe, Harry, and Grace—for the many ways in which they contribute to my books, my writing, and my writing life.